INITIATION

Initiation

This is a work of fiction. The author has invented the characters. Any resemblance to any persons, living or deceased is purely coincidental.

Cover Design by Olatunji
Interior Design by Salt

RockWrite Publishing along with Rose-Atrum Empire trade paperback printing 2023.

For more information, or to contact the author, send correspondence to: sthegemini69@gmail.com

Salt

Acknowledgments

To the Most High, I simply say thank you. To those who supported Initiation when it was first written in 2010 or 2011, I thank you, the full story is finally here!!

To the best new cousins, accountability and business partners a person could ask for, Joe and Kamaloni, I THANK YOU AND LOVE Y'ALL TO LIFE!! This is only the beginning and it's nothing but up from here!!

Last but not least, to all the freaks, the uninhibited ladies and gentlemen who love sex just as much as I do, this one's for you!

One question for you, who's ready to get down and dirty and join Beta Delta Mu and Delta Pi Psi?! If interested in joining, please send an email to sthegemini69@gmail.com

Nastiee Girl Salt signing out!!

Salt

Initiation

Salt

Every woman deserves a man that can make her cum multiple times a day in multiple ways. I am that man ~ Pussy Monster.

Making women scream, cream, squirt and cum is a gift. I can make women wet by just looking at them. When I finish with women, they are pure faucets ~Waterboi.

Initiation

Salt

Initiation

Initiation

"Justice baby, keep hittin' that spot there baby! Oh, My Gawd!! You're about to make me cum!!"

"Baby, your pussy is so damn wet! Where can I bust this nut?"

"Don't pull out, please, let's cum together," Akira said before another orgasm ripped through her body.

"Ahhhhhhhhh!!!" Akira and I screamed at the same time as we climaxed together.

"Kira, there's no way ya pops will let you go to school down south?"

"Nope, I've begged, pleaded, and even tried to reason with him, it's a no-go bae."

"Damnit, what does ya moms think about you going to school out of state?"

"She's all for it, she's even been talking to my father about it for me but he's just not budging. I kinda think he knows if I move down south for school I'm not coming back here to live."

Initiation

"Fuck! So, what are we going to do about us? You know staying in Connecticut after school for me was never the plan, but I don't want to leave you."

"Do you think we can make a long-distance relationship work? Or do you think we should just go our separate ways? I don't want you to feel obligated to me while you're down south."

"Kira, I plan on marrying you once we graduate so breaking up is not an option for me. I think if we both want the relationship to work, we can do the long-distance thing."

"You really want to marry me?"

"I'd marry you tomorrow if I could love. I think we've decided then; we'll visit one another during our breaks and if your parents will allow it, I can spend Thanksgiving here with you and for Christmas break you can come to Georgia and spend it with Jay and I."

"I'm with it; I really think we can make it work; communication will be key in making it work bae."

"We'll be aight, maybe after a year or so ya pops will loosen his grip on you and you'll be able to transfer, either way, you're stuck with me," I told Kira while playfully hitting her on her ass.

Initiation

Two months later in Atlanta

"Bruhhhhhhhh, Atlanta is more than I ever imagined! And do you see the women down here? Got damn!"

"Jay, the last thing on my mind is the women down here, did you forget I'm with Akira? She's my one and only, the only one I have my eyes on."

"You sound whipped J; I'll just have to have enough fun for the both of us while we're down here."

"As long as you keep up with your grades, I don't give a damn how much fun you have, just remember our end goal is to get that diploma."

"Yea, yea, you know when it comes to the edumacation, I got that on lock, so don't even worry. I do remember what mama and daddy had in their will regarding our inheritance, I'm only two minutes younger than you boy."

Salt

"Just know that our inheritance is dependent on both of us walking that stage and getting our diplomas. So, if one of us fucks up, we fuck it up for the both of us."

My brother and I sat in silence for what seemed like an eternity, we had never really spoken about the loss of our parents to anyone, not even amongst ourselves, it was rather difficult to discuss, even with each other. Just a quick backstory on our parents' untimely passing, it was the summer leading up to me and Jay's senior year in high school. One of our cousins had a going away party for his son's departure to college. My parents were lightweights when it came to drinking and for some reason or another, they thought they'd be able to hang with our cousins who drink any day that ends in y and any time that ends with o'clock or thirty. Either way, after my parents were rather saucy, they thought it would be a good idea to take the hour drive back home but never made it; they merged onto the highway going the wrong way and an eighteen-wheeler collided with them before either driver had time to break or try to avoid the accident. My parents were killed instantly, and because of their prior investments and good choices in business, it left our brother and I with more than enough money to pay for their funeral, bury them, pay for their headstones, and still live comfortably and a bonus, they left us both a hefty inheritance that we can only receive once we get our college degrees.

"You good J? You got quiet and started staring off."

I wiped a tear from my eye and replied, "yea, I'm good, just can't believe mama and pops won't be here to see us get our degrees again, it didn't seem real at our high school graduation and it's not going to seem real when we walk for our college graduation either."

"It sucks big time bro, to the point where I almost don't want to drink anymore, just imagining the scene of the accident still gives me nightmares and remembering when the state troopers came to the house to tell us the horrible news," JayVon said wiping tears from his eyes.

"One thing for sure and two for certain, we got through it all with each other, and we'll continue to have each other's backs as we get through life without our parents. They've instilled a lot of knowledge, positivity, and great values in us, so we'll be good."

"True indeed, but enough of this sad talk, let's see what this campus has to offer before classes start later this week."

JayVon and I locked up our apartment and decided to see what Atlanta University's campus had to offer. When we got to the campus, different Greek organizations had booths for perspective pledges, all the D9 orgs were out in full swing, the Ques were strolling, the Deltas were strolling, it was amazing, but there were a group of guys that had on their organizations paraphernalia but had no booth, they stood out to me the most, they caught my brother's eye too.

The organization's name was Beta Delta Mu, they donned black jackets with red and gold writing, one thing I do know for sure is that they aren't a part of the Divine 9, which is why I think they stood out to my brother and me.

"J, do you see what I'm seeing?"

"If you're talking bout the brothers of Beta Delta Mu, yea, I peeped them as soon as we came out here. You thinking what I'm thinking?"

"If you're thinking we should see if they're having an interest meeting soon, hell yea! There's something different about them than the other organizations, and I like being different."

"I'm with you! Let's go see what they say."

My brother and I walked over and introduced ourselves, a brother by the name of Bro. DipStick greeted us and told us if we were interested in learning more about the fraternity to give him our contact information and two hours before the informational, we'd receive a text message with where to be. We thought it was a bit odd but since they piqued our interest, we went along with it.

Three days later, just as I was leaving my photography class, I got a text message with an address and a message that read 'meet us at the above address within the next hour and a half, turn your location on so we'll know when you have arrived.

"An hour and a half gives me enough time to shower, get dressed and get there," I said to myself.

Just as I was getting back to our apartment, my brother came right behind me.

"Did you get the text message too?" JayVon asked me.

"Yea, we need to shower, get dressed and be on our way, no time to bullshit."

Initiation

"I already know what I'm wearing, and according to the GPS, it's twenty minutes from here and you know Atlanta traffic is like New York, so we gotta move it so we won't be late."

"Say less."

Jay and I pulled up with ten minutes to spare, one thing about us, we hated arriving somewhere right on time, which is something we got from our mother. When we got there, there were three other guys waiting to be let in.

"What's good fellas? I'm Justice, this is my twin brother JayVon."

"Peace king, I'm Daron," replied the one who was tall as the fuck.

"What's good Bruh, I'm André," replied another.

"What up y'all, I'm Levi, nice to meet y'all."

JayVon replied, nice to meet y'all. I thought for sure there'd be more people here."

"So did we, Levi replied.

Just as Brotha DipStick was opening the door, another brotha was running up.

"My bad on my tardiness, " he said to Brotha DipStick, "I'm Xavier", he said to the rest of us.

We each dapped him up and followed Brotha DipStick into a room where there were about five or six other guys from Beta Delta Mu.

"Welcome gentlemen, I am Brotha LDLT, tonight you will be given general information about Beta Delta Mu Fraternity, Incorporated, and then we'll open the floor up for you guys to ask any questions you may have."

Xavier immediately raised his hand, and all of us were looking at him like bruh, how do you have a question already and we ain't even been here ten minutes.

Initiation

Brotha LDLT looked at Xavier and then said to the room, "please keep all questions until the end of the presentation."

Xavier immediately put his hand down and seemingly had an attitude about being ignored.

"As most of y'all noticed three days ago Beta Delta Mu was the only org that hadn't set up a table, and reason being, we draw those to us who we feel and believe are supposed to be a part of our organization. We have had many guys come to an informational only to realize that BDM was not the right fit for them and for that, we hold no grudges. Every organization is not for everyone, and we take things up a couple of notches in Beta Delta Mu, some of the other fraternities may be nasty, we get downright dirty. Beta Delta Mu was founded right here on the campus of Atlanta University in 1914 by five men who realized none of the other fraternities were what they were looking for. You will not find the members along the walls of any of the buildings here on campus because of our exclusivity and because some members of the administration team were trying to get the fraternity shut down until they realized one of the founders was one of the administrators. Beta Delta Mu is an exclusive erotic fraternity, we love sex, and we love pleasing women in all ways imaginable. We do not condone under any circumstance sexual harassment or abuse of any women, even if they are our significant others. During the initiation process, you will be required to performance certain sexual acts with women whom we have chosen and who understand their roles in which we operate. If you gentlemen have significant others, this is something you may consider not discussing with them as everything that goes on in Beta Delta Mu is the business of Beta Delta Mu's brothers only. Oh, before I forget to mention it, once you cross, a selected few will be chosen down the line to cross into our elite division, but that's a while down the road. Lastly, does anyone have family members who are a part of Beta Delta Mu? If you do that's one way to almost guarantee you get in. Any questions or comments?"

Xavier didn't bother to say anything, he just got up and left. I looked at JayVon and he looked at me and we simultaneously said, "and then there were five."

Brothers LDLT and DipStick just laughed, then DipStick looked at the five of us and said, "I think y'all will make it through, how long has everyone known one another?"

Daron said, "we just met this evening, but I can almost be certain we're going to get along just fine."

Brother LDLT replied, "trust me when I say this, if y'all make it through this together, y'all will be family instead of just fraternity brothers. Oh, there is one other brother I want to introduce to y'all, he came to an informational a few days ago and he was the only man left standing, so I'm going to have him come in with y'all."

"Hey fellas, my name is Julius, freshman here at Atlanta University, and my major is business management. I'm looking forward to building with y'all and becoming brothers through Beta Delta Mu."

We all embraced him and the six of us chopped it up for another ten minutes or so before heading back to our respective places.

"J, what'd you think of tonight?"

"I'm excited to pledge, but even more excited to build with those brothas, seems as if we may have some of the same classes as Julius, seeing as though we're all majoring in business management. What are your thoughts?"

"I'm pumped, the guys seem to have good heads on their shoulders, and they seem cool as fuck too. Are you going to mention this to Akira?"

"Yea I am, maybe after we cross, I don't want to hear shit from her father, you know he's one of those holier than thou pastors, and when he finds out I'm in a fraternity, an erotic one at that, he's going to tell Akira she's basically too good for me."

"I don't see how you deal with that dude yo, couldn't be me. She is an only child too? That means he doesn't have anyone else to put his focus on but Kira. More power to you bro, you are more patient than me."

"I'm invested bro, despite her father being a bit too much at times, she's going to be your sister-in-law after we graduate, so the pastor is going to have to accept it."

Two weeks later

"Alright gentlemen, being as though there are only six of y'all, this initiation process won't take too long. There will be long nights ahead of you, and even longer days, so sleep when you can and be sure to maintain your grades, education is our top priority, and we can't and won't allow anyone to online and not keep up with their grades. By the end of the initiation, you will or should know the fraternity's history, our mission statement, and our values. Oh, has anyone found out whether they have family members in BDM?" Brotha LDLT asked.

"We are going to ask some of our family members, we lost our parents a little over a year ago and to our knowledge, neither one of them were a part of any organizations, but we should know something by the time we meet again," JayVon replied.

"Damn, we send our condolences bro, that shit can't be easy, just know we're here for you should you need anything," Bro. DipStick replied.

Then Levi chimed in, "If I'm not mistaken, my grandfather was a member of BDM, is there any way we can look up members who have passed away?"

"Yea, we can help y'all look into that; having family that is or was in the fraternity will be a great look for y'all, even better if they're still alive and can write letters of recommendation."

Initiation

Brothas DipStick and LDLT talked with us a few more minutes before they adjourned the meeting. As always, Levi, Julius, JayVon, André, Daron and I stayed a little while longer and talked. "Sorry to hear about your parents, that shit can't be easy to handle," Daron said.

"Not at all and to lose then both at the same time really fucked us up but in the same breath, it made us stronger. I don't think either of us knew the strength we possessed until we had no choice but to be strong for one another and handle everything," JayVon replied.

It became silent for a good minute before André broke the silence, "what dorm is everyone staying in?"

Julius replied, "I'm in Marshall."

Levi, André, and Daron all replied at the same time, "so am I."

"We got a house off campus," I told them.

"That's even better, cause if it's alright with y'all, your place would be the perfect spot for us to meet up at and go over this fraternity history, get this stuff embedded in our heads," André said.

JayVon replied, "That's fine with us, gives us all a chance to get to know one another better and if there's things that we need to do for this initiation and have to be under the radar, our spot is definitely the best spot."

"Say less, when is everyone free? We can all agree on a mutual time and get together."

"Does anyone have classes on Fridays? My brother and I don't have any classes on Fridays."

"I have one class at like eight in the morning on Fridays, after that I'm free until Mondays," Levi replied.

The rest of the guys were free on Fridays as well, so we all agreed that this coming Friday we'd link up and help one another study the history, mission statement and values of Beta Delta Mu.

One week later

Bro. DipStick opened the meeting, "ok gentlemen, you all have really surprised us with how quickly you've memorized the history, values, and mission statement of Beta Delta Mu, now the fun part begins. I hope none of y'all are married cause it's about to get real nasty for the next few weeks. As we've said before, other organizations may be known for being nasty, but let me tell y'all, they are not on our level of nasty, so even though y'all are in it, I'm going to ask one last time, if you think this is not the right frat for you, you can exit now and there will be no hard feelings."

We all looked at one another to see if anyone was going to bounce, and as I suspected, we were in this for the win.

"Ok, so now that I know y'all are serious, let's get this thing started. First and foremost, I must reiterate this, anything, and everything we discuss and or do must not be told, you must not tell anyone you are pledging Beta Delta Mu. At the end of the initiation process, we will hold a probate in the quad to present you all. Oh, and before we end tonight's meeting, you will be given burner phones that will be exclusively for the purpose of communication for Beta Delta Mu business. We are going to meet with you all individually to get to know you on a more personal level, and soon after, you will have your line names. JayVon, you're up first."

One by one Brotha DipStick called us into another room to talk to us, and while one of us was in the other room, Brotha LDLT handed out the burner phones. To say we were slightly nervous about what the initiation process entitled would be an understatement but in the same breath, we were excited to be a part of a brotherhood and gain lifetime connections. Once all of us had met with Brotha DipStick our meeting was adjourned.

A week later

Initiation

Four o'clock in the morning and me and JayVon's phones start ringing alerting us that we had a message. We looked at our phones and read the message simultaneously out loud. "Ok gentlemen, in your phones are the names and numbers to the ladies who are going to help you get through this initiation process. Two ladies are on their way to each of you and whatever their fantasy is with you guys, you must oblige. Have fun, be safe and be discreet, I know some of y'all are in dorm rooms so try not to be too loud."

"J, I think we should have the guys come over here with the ladies, just in case things get a little rowdy, none of them will get in trouble for having company and for being too loud."

"Totally agree with you, I'll shoot them a text, before I hop in the shower."
Just as Jay was getting out of the shower, our doorbell rang and when I opened the door, there were two goddesses standing there in a trench coat

and pumps, my dick sprang straight up in my sweatpants.

"It looks like someone is ready to play tonight, the taller of the two said as she licked her lips."

"Come on in ladies, make yourselves comfortable, can we offer you anything?"

"Only thing we are here for is hard dick and a damn good time."

"We definitely have hard dick on the menu for you ladies," Jay said as he joined us in just his shorts.

"Damn, I never fucked twins before, this is going to be better than I expected," the shorter of the two said.

"Ladies, please accept our apologies, my name is Justice, and this is my brother JayVon."

"Nice to meet you, my name is Alika, and this is my cousin Natalia."

Both women stood up and took their coats off, I love Akira, but these women were bad as fuck, probably the baddest women I've ever laid eyes on. Alika had on a lime green bra and panty set with what looked to be about a size 38 DD breast size, I couldn't wait to have her titties all over my face and dick. Natalia took her coat off too and she was on the slim side, but she had ass and tits for days, their bodies were southern bred and fed. Just as Jay and Natalia were on their way to his bedroom, there was another ring at our door, it was the rest of the guys with their females. I don't know where the brothas found these women but believe me when I tell you, there was not one busted looking chick here.

"Welcome fellas, and ladies, make yourselves comfortable wherever you'd like, there is ample room for everyone to be comfortable and if you'd like a little more privacy, there are extra rooms both upstairs and downstairs for your choosing," I told everyone before being pulled into the bathroom by Alika.

Alika turned on the shower, made sure the temperature was just right then said to me, "get in daddy, I want to watch you stroke your dick while you stand in the shower, and I'm going to sit right here on the sink and watch you watch me finger this wet pussy of mine, then, I want us to cum together before I join you."

Hearing Alika talk that freaky shit made my dick jump and grow harder. I stepped into the shower, never taking my eyes off Alika. She started off slowly rubbing her clit, then as my strokes became faster, she rubbed her clit faster, then inserted two fingers into her wet pussy all the while staring at me in the showering while I was stroking my dick. After a good ten minutes she began shaking uncontrollably and watching her make herself climax made me climax, I shot my man potion into the shower, then stepped out.

"Do you mind if I suck your dick?"

"Hell, no I don't mind."

Initiation

"Can you fuck me in my ass after I suck your dick? I love anal sex."

"Your wish is my command."
This chick was a bona fide freak, I've been with my share of women but none of them have ever let me fuck them in the ass. Alika stepped in the shower, I followed behind her, then she got on her knees and went to town on my dick, for a split second, I thought about taking a break with Akira, a mouth like Alika's need not go to waste.

••

In the room with JayVon and Natalia

"What's your favorite part of sex Natalia?"

"Believe it or not, I love giving head just as much as I love getting it, and I love recording my sessions."

"Say no more," I placed a towel on the bed, Natalia laid on it, and pressed record on her small camcorder. I slid two fingers into her pussy, took them out and tasted her, she tasted like pineapples. I slid her panties off her and tossed them, I was ready to devour. I gently licked her clitoris, then kissed the inside of both of her thighs. I allowed my tongue to enter her sweet wet pussy, before I was able to suck on her clit she began shaking uncontrollably, then she squirted all over my face, we were going to have a lot of fun tonight. I kept my mouth on her as she was squirting, I wasn't a quitter and I'm not one to let up when a woman is enjoying my mouth on her. Natalia came five times before she started tapping my shoulder.

"Jay, allow me to return the favor, you've outdone yourself tonight," she told me out of breath.

I grabbed a new towel from my closet as the one she was laying on was soaked; took my sweatpants off then, laid on the new towel and she handed me her camcorder.

My dick was already hard from eating her out, so she wasn't starting this head session from scratch, if you get my drift.

"Damn!" she yelled as she saw my dick standing straight up.

Initiation

"What's wrong?"

"Nothing is technically wrong, I've just never seen a dick as thick and long as yours, that's all."

"If you don't feel comfortable with it you can give me a hand job instead, I don't want to make you uncomfortable in any way.

"We can at least try to fuck after I attempt to fit it in my mouth, and I appreciate you trying to ease my anxiety, I've truly never seen or fucked a man with a dick as big as yours."

I pressed record on the camcorder and watched as Natalia attempted to give me head. I tried to help her out, but she seemed to be struggling and embarrassed.

With tears coming out of her eyes, she said to me, "I'm sorry Jay, I can't seem to please you tonight, I'm going to get my things and go, but please promise me you won't tell LDLT and DipStick that I couldn't perform tonight."

Salt

I turned the camera off, wiped her tears and lifted her face so she could look me in my eyes and told her, "Listen, I'm not here to snitch on anyone and who said you weren't able to please me? Me watching you squirm, squirt, shiver and shake was more than enough for me, I get pleasure from watching my partner being pleased by me. You have nothing to worry about Natalia, everything that happened between us tonight is between us, no one else has to know about it, you have my word."

"I appreciate you Jay, I really do." Natalia began to get dressed, put her shoes and coat back on before leaving my room.

I put my sweatpants back on, threw a wife beater on and walked her to the living room. Just as we made it to the living room, Alika and Justice were walking in as well and Alika was looking like she was taken on the ride of her life. Justice and I both walked the ladies to their car, hugged each of them and watched them drive off.

Initiation

When we got back in the house, we noticed the rest of the guys and the ladies had made themselves quite comfortable in the living room.

Justice says to them, "since it's late, early, or whatever you want to call it, y'all can crash here if you don't feel like driving back to campus."

"Oh no, we can't stay the night, the brothas would have our asses if they knew we didn't leave, but we do appreciate the hospitality," replied the chick who was with André.

"Fair enough, we just want to make sure y'all are good to drive home."

"We got a ride over here and our ride should be here any second now to pick us up," said the same chick.

"Ok, cool, well, guys, if y'all don't feel like driving back to campus tonight you're more than welcome to stay here."

"You ain't gotta tell me twice," Levi said. The guys walked the ladies to their car, watched them pull off before coming back into the house.

"If you want to shower, there is a guest shower on each floor, face, and body towels as well as body wash in the bathrooms under the sink, help yourselves. I have an eight o'clock class so I'm going to shower and try to get a few hours of sleep," I told them.

"I'm right there with you brotha," Julius stated.

We all went our separate ways, when I tell you tonight was a hell of a night, it was, but if our initiation process was going to be anything like tonight, then yea, sign me up for all of it!

A Week Later

Brothas DipStick and LDLT called a special meeting, and when we got there, we noticed it was only me, JayVon, and Levi.

"What's good guys?" Brother DipStick asked.

"Nothing much, how are you?"

"I can't complain. Listen, I'm not going to hold y'all too long, I just wanted to let you know I looked into the lists of last names y'all gave me to see if any of them may be related to you. Upon my research, I found out that your grandfathers were founding members of the fraternity, so between you and me, y'all are as good as in already, and if anyone finds out afterwards that you have a direct link to this fraternity, you're going to be treated like royalty."

JayVon and I looked at one another with our eyebrows raised, we had no clue we had family that was about that Greek life.

Levi asked, "So, does this mean that we don't have to finish the initiation process?"

"That's exactly what it means, unless you just want to, and that's totally up to you, but between the four of us, y'all are in already. I printed out the information on your grandfathers just in case you wanted to read it," Dipstick replied, handing the three of us a folder.

"We'll continue to send you all the text messages for your initiation until you tell us

otherwise, have a great evening gentlemen,"
Brotha DipStick said before leaving.

Levi, JayVon and myself looked at one
another, then JayVon said to Levi, "yo, you know
this means we are basically family now, right?
Like you are our damn brother!"

"Hell yea! Now we have to meet each
other's families, where are y'all originally from?"

"Connecticut", I replied, then said, "Where's
your family from?"

"New York, Brooklyn to be exact."

"Damn, we've been neighbors this whole
time and it took us to get to Georgia for us to
connect, that's crazy."

"Hell yea it is, but I will say this, the best is
yet to come from us connecting through this
fraternity and even with the news we found out
tonight."

"True indeed brotha, listen, we plan on
heading home for a quick weekend trip the week

after next, if you want to roll with us, you're more than welcome to.

"I think I'll take you up on that.

"I don't know about y'all but I'm 'bout to go back to the crib and go through this envelope full of newfound information," JayVon said to us.

"I'm about to do the same", Levi stated."

"Shit, if you want, you can come through to our crib and we can go through all of this together."

"I think that's what I'll do, and maybe with some digging and research when we go back home, we can find some pictures or memorabilia from our OG's."

"Facts, well, I'm up outta here, I'm going to grab me something to eat before I get back to the crib, "JayVon told us while dapping us up.

• •
Three hours later

"Good evening gentlemen, I hope all is well with you all. We have heard nothing but great things about you all from the ladies you entertained during your first initiation event, now it's time for the next round. Some of the faces you see tonight will be familiar to you and others you will see for the first time as you all partake in a fuck fest if you will. You all will need to be at the address listed below by eleven o'clock tonight sharp so everything can be set up and ready when the women get here. Good luck and see y'all tonight."

"J, I'm not missing this shit tonight for anything in the world, a fuck fest? Fuckin' multiple women during however many hours we have to be there? I'm going to be in heaven with these freaks."

I laughed then said, "I knew you weren't going to miss this for anything in the world, this fuck fest tonight is right up your alley, enjoy yourself bruh."

"You're not coming tonight?"

"Nah, I'm going to sit this one out. I have some papers that need to be written for a few classes, plus I need to call Akira, we've been missing each other calls lately and I think she's starting to second guess this whole long distance relationship thing."

"Well, you do you bro and I'm going to bang as many of these chicks as I can tonight, I'll even get enough pussy for you too."

"Aight bro, have fun and make sure you wrap it up, I don't need six and seven nieces and nephews around here with four or five different mamas."

"You ain't funny," JayVon said with a chuckle, then said, "nah, no kids from me until I meet someone who can handle my sexual appetite, until then I will leave as many women mesmerized with my tool as I can."

"Sad thing is, I know you're so serious about getting these chicks sprung on your dick, you crazy bro."

"Well, I'll see you tomorrow kid, going to hop in the shower and get up outta here, tell my future sis in law that I said what up and can't wait to see her in two weeks."

"Be safe kid, love you and tell the guys I said what up."

** *Later that evening* **

"Welcome gentlemen, we're glad you all were able to find the hotel without any issues. As you can see, we have rented out this entire floor just for tonight's festivities, and because today is Friday and we know none of you have classes on Saturday's, that means you have more than enough time to engage in the fuck fest for more than one night. As you saw, most rooms come with either a king size bed or two twin beds, all rooms have a couch that pulls out into a bed, and a small kitchen, but I doubt anyone will be concerned with the kitchen tonight, but just in case you all decide to stay for the duration of the weekend, it's there for y'all to utilize," Brotha LDLT said to us right before the women began coming in.

Initiation

Brother DipStick then said, "Ladies, you know the drill, and gentlemen I shouldn't have to tell you this but if one of these women say no to anything, that's exactly what it means, no, as we've said in the very beginning, we don't condone sexual harassment or sexual misconduct in any form. We are all adults, so please, let's conduct ourselves as such, with that being said, let the festivities commence.

Natalia and Alika from a few nights ago both made eye contact with me at the same time, I smiled at them and opened my arms to them, it was about to go down!

"Ladies, so nice to see you again, I hope you're ready for a great time tonight."

Natalia replied, "We sure are, I don't see your brother, is he not here tonight?"

"Nah, he decided to stay home and get some work done tonight, so you ladies can share me if you'd like."

"I wouldn't mind tasting you tonight, shit, if you're anything like your brother, I'm in for a hell of a treat."

Alika looked at me with a bit of nervousness in her eyes.

"I promise to be a gentleman, and respect any boundaries you may have, now shall we go have some nasty fun?"

"Lead the way daddy," Alika replied.

I led the ladies to the first empty room I saw. Alika pushed me onto the bed and immediately sat on my face, I guess my tongue and hands left a lasting impression on her. While I was eating Alika out, Natalia took my pants off me, spit on my dick then took as much of it as she could fit into her mouth. I wasn't small by any stretch of the imagination so her being able to fit more than half of my dick in her mouth was impressive. The combination of her wet and warm mouth mixed with her massaging my balls with one hand and her other hand on my dick, she was trying to get me to bust quickly, but it wasn't happening.

Alika came at least six times from me eating her out and seeing her being pleased by mouth made my dick even harder.

"Alika, come get this dick and eat me out while he's fucking you."

I looked at Alika and she looked at me and nodded her head, I then knew she was willing to try my dick again.

"At any time, you feel uncomfortable, you just let me know, and please let me know if I'm hurting you at any moment."

"Ok Jay", were her only words.

Alika laid down, took a deep breath and I entered her wet, throbbing pussy.

"Fuckkkkkk," was the only word I was able to utter when I put the head of my dick into her.

"Keep going if you like, I can tolerate more."

"You sure?"

"Yes."

I went in a little deeper and her legs began shaking uncontrollably.

That's right baby, shake for daddy, I told her as her body kept shaking.

"Jay, what the fuck are you doing to me?"

"I hope I'm making you feel good, are you feeling good?"

"Yessss," she replied as another orgasm ripped through her body and then began squirting everywhere.

Little by little Alika got used to my dick's width and length and before I knew it, she was matching my thrusts with her hips, this was the Alika I wanted the other night at my crib.

"Damn Jay, I want to feel you inside of my pussy now, Alika can't be the only one who gets to experience you," Natalia said to me as she was fingering her pussy.

Alika's screams attracted more attention than I anticipated because as she and Natalia were changing positions, there were more and more women coming into our room to experience me. I was on a high and if these women kept coming in, I was going to do whatever I had to, to make sure they were pleased.

"Well damn, all of y'all in here to experience this dick?"

"We're here to experience your dick, your tongue and each other sexy," one of the women replied.

I didn't see who replied, but I would know her by her voice. As Alika and Natalia traded places, three other women joined us on the bed and they began eating each other out and fingering one another, I swear I died and went to sex heaven. This one chick caught my eye for real though, shorty was bad as fuck, like slim, thick, rocking her natural hair, which was thick and curly, she had it all in a ponytail except for her bangs. We locked eyes, she smiled and winked at me, I needed to know who she was, and I needed to know now.

Salt

Natalia took my dick in her mouth before I started fucking her, this girl was talented, she surprised me. As she was done topping me off, she took my dick, put the condom on with her mouth, then put my dick in her pussy herself, as soon as I was in her, she gasped and said, "you and your brother are huge, my pussy might not be right after tonight."

I laughed and said, "I bet you'll never forget us, we like to leave lasting impressions, now shut up and take this dick."

With each thrust of mine, Natalia was in sync, matching my rhythm and when she locked eyes with me, that's when I lost it, I came long and hard.

"Ahhhhhh!!" I let out a grunt, that nut was long overdue.

"Does this mean you're done for the night?" The mystery woman asked.

It was the woman I had my eyes on, the slim, thick shorty with the natural hair.

Initiation

"No sweetheart, as long as you ladies can get him up, I'll be here to service all of you until you can't take anymore."

Shorty came and started licking on my chest while her perfectly manicured hands began massaging my dick and balls.

"Come lay down so I can get him back up just so I can put him back down," she told me.

I put up no fight, I found a spot on the bed, and laid down as she began spitting on my dick and giving me a hand job. Another woman came and sat on my face, she was petite and cute, but my head was still on shorty who had my dick in her mouth…

Back at the house with Justice…

One paper down, two more to go, but before I start the next, let me see what my baby girl is up to.

"Hey handsome, I was just thinking about you, how are you?"

Salt

"I'm good love, how are you? How's school going?

"School is school, I changed my major from journalism to business management with a minor in entrepreneurship."

"What made you change your major?"

"I've been thinking about it for a while, and some of the girls in my dorm were talking about their plans after graduation, and basically solidified my thoughts about changing my major. I'm also taking photography classes as well; I think it'll be a great asset."

"I'm proud of you baby girl, what did your parents think about you changing your major?"

"They don't even know about it, don't even think they really care, as long as I get my degree, they'll be happy."

"Do what makes you happy love. You know I miss you right?"

"I know and I miss you too. Can't wait to see you"

"Oh, I didn't tell you, Jay and I are coming down the weekend after next, we'll be leaving Thursday after our last class and coming back on Sunday evening, so you'll be seeing me real soon love."

"Is everything alright?"

"Everything is fine, we're coming to check on the house, link with some family members and handle some other business."

"Shall I book a room for us?"

"Nah, you don't have to, you can stay at the house with us, it's only going to be the three of us, unless Jay decides to bring someone."

"Ok, love, well, my girls and I are about to head out for a little while, I can't wait to see you when you touch down."

"Text me when you get back in, I'll be up."

"Is everything alright? I can stay in and talk if you need me to."

"Talking isn't what I want to do later," I told her with a smirk on my face.

"Only you," she responded while laughing.

"He's already at attention just from hearing your voice."

"See, you're about to make me stay in and make a video just for you. She's wet and throbbing right now, damn I wish you were here right now. I miss feeling you inside of me."

"I miss being inside of you baby, kissing you while I'm deep inside, feeling you squeezing and pulling me inside even more."

"You're about to make me book a flight to Atlanta right now with the way you're talking to me."

"If you do that, you won't be going back to New Haven, you'll be transferring to Atlanta University."

"Don't tempt me, I'll start packing my bags tonight. Can you do me a favor?"

"Anything for you love name it."

"Take him out for me."

Initiation

I did as she asked, "now what do you want me to do?"

"Imagine me sitting right in front of you, one hand gripping my breasts and the other fingering my pussy. Can you imagine that?"

I began stroking my already hard dick, "I sure can baby, while you have one of your breasts in your hand, I'm sucking on the other just like you like it, can you feel me?"

"Yes baby, I can feel you. Now, I want you to imagine me putting two fingers into my already wet pussy, all the while my eyes are locked on you, do you love it when I finger myself?"

"Oh, my gawd, yes baby, finger fuck that pussy for me baby," I told her with my raspy voice, as I started stroking my dick quicker.

"J, you're about to make me cum all over myself. J! I'm squirting everywhere, oh my goodness!"

"Fuckkkkkk Akira!" I yelled as I came with her.

The phone went silent for a good ten seconds, all you could hear was the both of us breathing heavily.

"Hey love, my girls are knocking at my door, your ass better be awake when I get in later, I'm going to video chat you, I need to see you stroking that dick."

"I'll be up, you better remember to call me when you get back in, and don't forget you got a man when you step out tonight."

"Me? Forget you? Never going to happen. you're stuck with me."

"And you're stuck with me. Go have a good time with your girls and I'll be looking forward to seeing you later through video. I love you baby girl."

"I love you too baby," Akira replied.

"I got half a mind to fly to Connecticut tonight just to get some pussy tomorrow," I said to myself. I knew I wasn't going to do it, but it was a thought in the front of my mind; I didn't realize how much I'd been missing Akira until just now, the week after next can't come soon enough.

The next evening

"Bruhhh, you missed a hell of a night last night and this morning, bitches galore! Those two freaks that were here with us the first night this initiation shit started, I took them both down, that freak you were with got some good head on her shoulders."

"Yo, why do you insist on calling women bitches? You are so disrespectful."

"It's the alcohol bro, you know I know better than that, we were raised better. Anyway, I had this one chick, shorty was bad as fuck! Like bad to the point where she could possibly be the one to get me to settle down."

"Get the fuck outta here! You settling down with one woman? I think you had too much to drink, 'cause you settling down with one woman would mean hell is freezing over."

Salt

"You're not funny, but in all seriousness, shorty was bad and there was something about her vibe that drew me to her. You know some of these chicks I wouldn't mind linking up with again just to fuck but that one shorty, I want to get to know her on a personal level, like on some we can do brunch or dinner type of shit."

"WOW! You're really serious about this chick. You've never talked about any other female like this before. What's her name? Where's she from?"

"I haven't the slightest clue, by the time things calmed down, she was gone, I'm going to text the bro's and see if they can get me her information. Shorty was bad though bro, slim, thick, natural hair, and like I said before, her energy was off the hook."

"It's worth a shot, all the bro's can say is either yes or no to giving you her contact information, good luck with that. I was on the phone with Kira last night, she told me to tell you hello and she can't wait to see you when we touch down."

"You told her we were coming?"

"Yea, why?"

"I thought we were going to hang with Levi and chill with the family, that's all."

"Unlike you, I'm in a committed relationship and again, unlike you, I'm not bouncing around from one pussy to the next, I need my fix from my baby. We're still going to hang with Levi and see what other family members are a part of Beta Delta Mu, and we gotta see if Pop Pop has any old photos at the house of him and his frat brothers. We'll have ample time to do everything, I know how to make time and prioritize everything and everyone in my life, unlike you."

"Yea, whatever, just don't go getting Kira pregnant on this trip, I'm not ready to be an uncle yet."

"Whatever, just make sure you're packed by Wednesday so we can leave on time Thursday evening."

"I got you, you're like mommy was, always early, never late and never right on time, I'll be packed by Tuesday. Cause I'm meeting up with Alika and Natalia again Tuesday evening after my last class, they asked about you too."

"Do you plan on going through the whole initiation process?"

"Yea, I want the full experience, how about you?"

"I was thinking about not, but then I thought about how I'd be missing the whole experience, so I decided to continue with it, this experience only happens once in a lifetime."

"True indeed, so we stickin' through this together, right?"

"We came into this world together, didn't we?"

"Always a smart ass."

"Have you spoken to Levi about it? Does he plan on sticking through until the end?"

"We haven't had an opportunity to speak about it, between classes, and this crazy weekend, I figured the best time to talk to him would be when we're on the way home, that way we don't have to worry about anyone else hearing anything, it'll be just the three of us in the car and we can speak freely."

"I feel you, you sure you want to drive instead of fly. Two and a half hours is a lot better and faster than fourteen hours and change."

"Honestly, it doesn't matter to me, if we decide to fly, we need to figure it out by tomorrow and let Levi know."

"Bet, I'll shoot him a text right now and see what he says, and you can start looking up flights."

"Aight, I'll let you know what I come up with."

I hit Levi up with a text message, "hey bro, may be a change of plans for the trip back home, instead of driving, we may be flying, Jay is looking up flights now."

He immediately responded, "shit, I thought we were flying the whole time, I was just about to hit y'all to see what time we were leaving."

"LOL, I guess I'm outnumbered, we shall fly back home. Jay is looking up flights now, so once we find something suitable for our schedules, we'll let you know, and we can book everything together."

"I just started a group text with the three of us and put the flights I found in the chat, if the times for departing Thursday and coming back Sunday evening work with y'all, I'll book them now and y'all just send me the money whenever."

"Speaking of a group chat, I don't know why no one started with all of us."

"Check your messages, we've started one, you've just been so busy with your classes that you haven't bothered checking your unread messages."

Initiation

"Oh shit, never even paid attention to them, I told him while looking through my messages."

"Figures," JayVon said to me, shaking his head and laughing.

One Month Later…Atlanta University Campus Quad

We were lined up, dressed in all black, we had masquerade type masks on, ready to make our debut.

"Okay gentlemen, tonight is the night you've worked so hard for. Tonight, is the night you can call yourselves men of Beta Delta Mu Fraternity Incorporated. We've kept things quiet and respectful for a couple of months now, now is the time to introduce yourselves to your peers," Brotha DipStick told us.

Brotha LDLT tapped JayVon on his shoulder then said, "introduce yourself."

Jay stepped forwards and said, "Every woman deserves a man that can make her cum multiple times a day in multiple ways; I am that man. I am Pussy Monster."

"Next!" Brotha LDLT yelled over the roaring crowd, the ladies were loving Jay and his intro.

I stepped to the front as Jay stepped back in line then said, "Making women cream, squirt and cum is a gift I don't take lightly. I can make women wet by just looking at them. I am Waterboi."

I stepped back into line, then Levi stepped up and said, "I was born to make a difference in women's lives. I'm educated, handsome and know how to use my dick in ways most brothers don't. My dick game is so dope, women propose to me. I am Demon Dick."

Levi stepped back, Julius stepped forward, "God made man in his perfect image, I'm his prototype. I can imagine the amount of ass he got from his angels. Because of him, I am here, here to please women, I'm not good at what I do, I'm great at it. I am Great Black Dick."

Daron then stepped forward, "Anal sex is sexy as fuck. Not every woman allows a man to enter her sacred hole, but every woman I've been with has allowed me to. I take my time with the ass, make sure she's comfortable before I assassinate that ass. I am Anal Assassin."

Lastly, André stepped forward, "I'm something like the full package and my package leaves women very full. My tongue leaves women in awe at what it can make their bodies do and feel. Some say my tongue is possessed and others say it's blessed, either way you look at it, my tongue is divine. I am Toxic Tongue.

The crowd was going sick, the ladies were screaming, throwing their clothes at us, it was pure pandemonium and I think I speak for my brothers when I say we were loving every moment of it.

After we finished introductions, we unmasked ourselves and the looks on some of the women's faces were priceless, especially the women who had classes with Jay and me. After probate was over, the big brothers decided to take us out, so we broke out in two separate cars and headed to the club.

As I'm driving my phone begins to vibrate, it's Akira. "Hey beautiful, how are you?"

"Hey handsome, I'm good, how are you? What's all that noise in the background?"

"I'm great love, I have not one complaint. That's Jay and some of our frat brothers, we're on our way to celebrate crossing into Beta Delta Mu tonight."

"Wait, you're in a fraternity? Why am I just now hearing about this?"

"Listen love, this is a conversation we can have face to face when I come home next weekend, I don't want to argue with you tonight."

"Whatever Justice," she replied before hanging up without allowing me to get another word in.

"Damn bro, wifey giving you trouble? I'm sure there will be some baddies at the club tonight to help you get your mind off her," Levi said.

"I'm not even on that type of time, I feel bad enough for fuckin' around on her during the initiation process, ain't happening again. When I touch down in Connecticut next weekend we're going to talk, and everything will be fine.

"Yo, y'all going back home next weekend? You mind if I tag along? I found out that I have family in Wallingford, how far is that from where y'all are?

"You know you just like family, no need to ask, and Wallingford is like fifteen to twenty minutes from where we stay."

"Bet, I appreciate it, how long y'all staying?"

"It's going to be a quick weekend trip, flying in on Friday morning, and flying back out on Sunday evening."

"Bet, that works cause that Monday morning I have an interview with an advertising agency."

"Congrats bro!! Big shit poppin'!"

"Yo, what do you fellas think about going into business together after we graduate?"

"I'm down for it, we're all majoring in business with different minors that I'm sure we're going to need when we start the business. How about Sunday evening we all have a meeting at our crib and brainstorm."

"Sounds like a plan, Julius replied.

After we parked and walked to the front of the club, Brotha DipStick had a few words with one of the bouncers, then he escorted us into the club to one of the VIP sections. Bottle girls were coming left and right with different bottles of alcohol, I looked at Jay and he looked at me, we knew we were going to be taking it easy with the alcohol, we didn't want another tragedy like our parents.

Anyway, shortly after arriving at our VIP section there were about thirty women who seemed to have come out of nowhere, all they knew about us was that we had just crossed Beta Delta Mu and they wanted to party with us. Jay was halfway out of it, his phone was keeping him preoccupied, so I went over to make sure he was good.

"All these women here and you're all the way into your phone, you good?

"Yea, I'm good, one of chicks I took down during initiation keeps hitting my line, I fucked around and got her dickmatized and now she won't leave me alone."

"You going to see her tonight?"

"Nah, I'm good on her, she only wants me for my body."

"Yo, you stupid!"

"I'm serious bro, I'm tired of knocking down different broads every day, I'm ready to settle down like you and Akira."

The look on JayVon's face told me that he was serious about wanting to settle down, I never thought I'd see this day or hear those words come out of his mouth.

"I'm going to break out early, so I'll holla at you when you get home tonight."

"Nah bro, we came together and we leave together," I told him.

We said our goodbyes to all the bros, and we headed out.

Back in Connecticut

Fuckkkkk Akira!! Keep riding this dick baby.

Akira was bouncing up and down on my dick like she was an equestrian.

"You love this pussy don't you baby?"

"You know I do, just as much as you love this dick."

Yesssss, Jay, I love your dick, but I love you more!"

Initiation

In one swift move I flipped Akira on her back and got all up in her guts, moments later, we climaxed together, and I fell on top of her.

"Don't think for one minute that this session got you off the hook, we still have to talk about why you decided to pledge and not tell me."

"Akira, you know when dealing with pledging, it has to be kept a secret until our probate, which is why no one knew, including you, and if you decided to pledge a sorority, I know you have to do the same thing and I won't hold it against you."

"You know how my father is, I could never pledge to a sorority."

"Akira, I mean this with nothing but love, but how long are you going to allow your father's opinion to take over your life? You're grown, and you can't keep allowing his thoughts of you and how you decide to live your life to control you."

"Justice, he's my father and I respect him, and not to mention the fact that he's helping with the college bills that my scholarship doesn't cover."

"So basically, he dangles his money over your head so you can live by his rules? Cause that's what it sounds like to me."

"Fuck you, Justice!" she said before storming into my bathroom.

"Truth hurts Akira, that's why you're mad, what I said was the truth and both of us know it."

"It's not the truth, it's your dumb ass opinion and I'm done talking about it."

"Fine Akira, lock my door on your way out. Yo Jay! You home?

"Just walking in, what's up with you and Akira? She walked past me without speaking, y'all good?"

"Right now, hell no we ain't good. She got mad because I didn't tell her I was pledging BDM, and I told her that if she decided to pledge to a sorority that I would understand her not telling me until after her probate because things like this are so secretive."

"I'm not understanding the issue."

"She was like she would and could never pledge a sorority because of her pops and I told her she's too old for her father to still be controlling her life, and that's when she got pissed, I told her he dangles his money over her head and controls her life."

"Okay, but anyone that knows Akira and her pops knows that does she not notice that?"

"No, she doesn't, I told her the truth hurts and that's why she really has the attitude because I'm telling the truth that she doesn't want to hear."

"Damn, you just let her walk up on outta here?"

"Sure the fuck did, I'm not about to keep chasing after her spoiled ass, I'm tired of that shit."

"Listen, there's a party at ECU tonight, let's roll, Levi is already down to go, it might help you take your mind off this shit with you and Akira."

"You know I never turn down a good party! We going in BDM para?"

"I'm probably going to wear one of our shirts, I don't want to be an overkill."

"Feel you, well let me know which one you're wearing so I don't put the same one on. What time we rollin' out?

"I'm thinking we can leave around ten, it's only ten minutes away."

"Yea, ten minutes away but it's going to take us at least twenty minutes to find a decent parking space."

"You right, I forgot how terrible parking in New Haven is on the weekends."

***

As I was getting out of the shower my phone was ringing, it was Akira. I looked at it and decided not to answer. Tonight, I was going to have fun with my frat brothers. I'd return her call in the morning before we headed back to the airport.

Initiation

"Fellas, y'all ready to hear some crazy shit?" Levi asked us while walking into our house.

"Is it good crazy or bad crazy cause I've had enough bad crazy for one day today."

"You and wifey?

"Yup, anyway, what's up?"

"So, check this shit," he says as he pulls a picture out of his back pocket.

"Yo, that's our grandfather, and the couple standing next to them looks like our great grandparents but who's the guy standing next to him?"

"My grandfather."

"So, are you saying that we're related?"

"Yup, we're cousins, shocked the hell out of me too when I found out."

"Yo, that's crazy! How'd you find out?"
"My, rather our family in Wallingford, which is where I got this picture from. Every picture with my grandfather and our great grandparents, your grandfather was in them, so I finally asked who

this guy was, and they were like that's your uncle Brian, so we started doing some digging and that's when I came across this picture," he said while pulling another picture out of his back pocket.

"That's us in the hospital with granddad and mommy, I think the day after we were born, we have that same picture around here somewhere in one of these photo albums."

"This shit is crazy," JayVon said.
"We have some serious catching up to do and some new family members to meet sooner rather than later, but for now, let's pregame before this party and see how they party at ECU.

I poured shots for us, we toasted to newfound family, BDM, and life, then we downed our shots and headed out the door.

***

"Akira, isn't that your man over there with the other guys?"

"Yup, sure is."

"Well damn bitch, any other time you see your boo you get all giddy and start blushing, what's your problem?"

"Nothing, we just had an argument earlier and I'm still pissed at him. I don't even know how he knew about the party tonight; he didn't say anything to me about coming tonight."

"You ain't his mother, he ain't gotta run shit by you, you trippin', but enough about you and him, who is that fine brotha standing to his right?"

"That's JayVon, his twin brother."

"Oh, let's go over there, you need to introduce me!"

"Trice, I don't want him to see me here, go over and introduce yourself."

"Now you know the big sistas are watching and you know the rules, we have to be doubled up at all times."

"You owe me! Let's go."

"Wifey alert, Akira is on her way over here bro," Levi told me with a slight nudge.

"Good looks bro."

I saw Akira when we walked into the party but because of our argument earlier, I wasn't pressed to go talk to her. Just as she and some chick were on their way over to where we were standing, two other chicks grabbed their attention, and they went to see what she wanted.

"Yo, look at Akira and the other chick, y'all notice how they're dressed in black and white?"

"Yea looks like they're pledging a sorority. You see the chicks they're with? Those are Greek letters on their jackets, never heard of them though," Levi stated.

"I'm trying to look them up now and I can't find anything," Jay responded.

"I know this chick ain't pledging a sorority after our argument today."

"Looks like she is though bro," Jay responded, shaking his head.

"Listen, we gonna sit here and talk about your girl and what she may or may not be doing or we gonna party? I'm trying to enjoy these last few hours we have here before we head back to campus tomorrow," Levi said.

"Say less bro," I responded while heading to the dance floor.

The DJ started playing some hits from year 2000 and when Say I Yi Yi came on, the crowd went sick, two chicks came up to me and one started grinding on me and the other started feeling all up on me, I was going to hear about this later but for now, fuck it, I was enjoying myself. As the DJ faded out the Ying Yang Twins, Stoke You Up by Changing Faces came on and there were a group of women who seemingly came out of nowhere, rocking their pink, yellow and silver, their Greek letters read Delta Pi Psi.

"Y'all ever hear of Delta Pi Psi Sorority? I'm trying to look it up but keep coming up empty handed."

"Hell no, but think about it, when people look up Beta Delta Mu, they can't find anything, so maybe they're like BDM, a freaky ass female version of us."

"It's whatever," I told them with a shrug of the shoulders.

"Bruh, you think she really bout to pledge?" Levi asked me.

"It seems like it but with the convo we had this morning, it would be hypocritical of her, but it's her life. Y'all ready to go? This shit just killed my mood."

"Yea, let's go, I gotta go back out to Wallingford anyway to see the fam before we pull out tomorrow."

Levi, Jay, and I all left, as we were walking out of the party, we saw some guys in BDM apparel, so we flicked it up with them, followed each other on Instagram and we headed out.

"Yo why don't y'all roll with me out to Wallingford to meet the family."

JayVon responded, "I'm down."

"So, am I, they won't mind us coming, will they?"

"Nah, I hit them already and told them y'all will be coming with me, they can't wait to meet you."

We all rode out to Wallingford to meet our family we never knew existed, they were cool as hell, told us stories about us when we were younger, had photo albums galore of our parents and us when we were younger, it was crazy. We stayed about three hours as we needed to get back home to pack to make our way back to Atlanta in the morning. Before leaving, we took a ton of pictures and promised to keep in contact with them.

When I pulled up to the house Akira was sitting in her car in my driveway.

"Uh oh cuz, looks like you got something to handle," Levi said before getting out of the car and heading to his.

I replied, "I'm not even in the mood for her shit tonight to be honest, but yo, you need us to pick you up in the morning before heading to the airport?"

"Nah, I was going to see if it's alright for me to park my car in your garage, I don't want to leave it where it's been."

"That's no problem, it's big enough."

"Appreciate it, I'll see y'all in the morning."

As Levi was pulling off, Akira was walking up the stairs.

"What's up?"

"Can we talk?"

"Yea."

"I didn't expect to see you at the party tonight."

"Well, Jay wanted to go so we went."

"Cool. I wanted to come see you, but I got pulled away to handle some things."

"I noticed."

"Are you going to keep answering me with one word?"

"What do you want from me, Akira?"

"Do you still love me?"

"You know I do; I just can't do the bullshit attitude with you constantly. It was cute in the beginning when we first met but now, it's tiring."

"I apologize for how I acted earlier, I was wrong, and I don't want you to go back to Georgia with us not on good terms."

"We good."

"Do you want me to stay the night?"

"Nah, I'm good, we gotta be up and out early to catch our flight back to Atlanta."

"I can help you pack and help you relax before your flight."

"Akira, I think we need to take a break for a little while, focus on college and if we're meant to be we will be together."

"Are you serious right now Justice?"

"Akira, are you pledging to a sorority?"

"I was but I just dropped out tonight."

"So, all your bullshit earlier today about me being secretive and joining a fraternity without you knowing, and here you were doing the same thing."

"I know, which is why I came over to apologize to you. Had I known you were going to be at the party tonight I would've told you ahead of time that I was trying to join a sorority."

"This is the shit I'm talking about! You were pissed at me for joining a fraternity and you not knowing until after I crossed and here you are doing the same thing; and you telling me ahead of time if you would've known about me coming to the party tonight, does that make any sense to you?"

"Yo, I really think we need to take some time apart, you need to figure out if this relationship is something you want to continue or if you would be better off single and we can just go our separate ways."

"Justice, I love you and we plan on getting married, do you really want to end things right now?"

"Just until you get your priorities straight, and when you figure out what you want and how to handle life like an adult, we can try again. You know I love you and I want to marry you but you gotta get your shit together. I think our relationship is a distraction to you and I don't want to be a distraction, so we can take some time apart and do what we do, focus on school and hopefully somewhere down the line, we can reconnect and get back together."

She began crying uncontrollably, which I knew was bound to happen but us taking a break from one another was something that needed to be done. If Delta Pi Psi was anything like Beta Delta Mu, she needed to take this break as a positive thing and realize that it's for the betterment of us and our relationship.

"If that's how you feel Justice then I have no choice but to respect it, I wish you the best."

"As I wish you the best as well and I hope you know this doesn't mean that we can't keep in contact, you're not getting rid of me that easy baby girl."

I gently grabbed her face and kissed her deeply, then picked her up, walked into the house and placed her on the couch. She began undressing and I did the same. I sat on the couch, and she straddled me and rode me like this was going to be the last time we ever made love.

We climaxed together after a good thirty minutes of intense love making, then Akira yelled out "FUCK!!"

"What's wrong?"

"I'm ovulating right now, I didn't realize it until just now when I checked my calendar. You know I like to stay away from you when I'm ovulating because we don't always use protection. I don't know how I missed it this time, fuck!"

Initiation

"Let's not panic, wait a few weeks then take a pregnancy test, then when we get the results, we'll know how to proceed."

"What do you mean we? If I'm pregnant this is my problem, not yours."

"Are you fuckin' kidding me right now Akira? If you are pregnant, that baby is just as much my responsibility as it is yours, we're in this together, you should know that by now."

"This is too much for me, I'll let you know what the test results say if I miss my next period."

I sat next to her and held her face in my hands and said to her, "baby girl, if today is the beginning of our parenthood journey, then you know I'm going to be by your side every step of the way, what more do I have to say or do to ensure you of that?"

"I don't know Justice, I think I'm more scared than anything, we're closing in on our first year of college, we're in two different states, and not to mention that if I am pregnant, you know my father is going to kick me out of the house and disown my ass, what am I going to do then?"

"We will figure it out, even if it means me transferring to ECU, you can move in here and we can turn one of the bedrooms into the nursery for the baby; I told you, we will be fine."

"Well, I'll know in about two weeks or so, and as soon as I find out, I'll let you know," she said while putting her clothes on and heading to the door.

"You're not driving home as late as it is so don't even think about it. You still have clothes in my dresser and all your toiletries are in the bathroom, so let's get comfortable in bed so we can get some sleep."

"You sure you're going to get some sleep with me here?"

"No I'm not but I'm going to try, cause I have to get up a little earlier now to pack my things before heading to the airport."

Initiation

"I can pack your things tonight so you can jump in the shower."

"I can get used to this, don't start spoiling me."

"Whatever, so, are you planning on staying in Georgia for the summer or are you coming back to Connecticut?"

"I actually have a business meeting with my line brothers when I get back tomorrow to discuss a business, we're thinking about starting after graduation. I was hoping after we graduated you would consider moving down there with me."

"I wouldn't mind that, you know I've been wanting to move out of Connecticut since last year."

"Good, but to answer your question, I planned on spending half the summer in Georgia and the other half in Connecticut, just found out earlier this evening that I have family I never knew in Wallingford so when I am up here, I want to be able to have time to spend with them to get to know them."

"That's what's up baby, I'm happy for you "

"Don't think you're getting off that easily though, I didn't forget you and that sorority you're trying to join, but we can have that discussion at another time."

"Duly noted love, you won't get an argument out of me."

I hopped in the shower while Akira packed my bags for me. As we were getting settled in bed, we heard Jay coming in with his latest conquest, I'm assuming it was some random chick from the party.

Four Years Later…Atlanta, Georgia

"Yo Jay! I know your punk ass sees me calling you, come open the door!"

"Damn bruh, can't even bust a nut in peace, you got the worst timing ever my guy!"

"My bad bro, but I wanted to see if you got the same letter in the mail that I got today from the fraternity."

"I haven't checked the mail yet, told you I've been busy trying to bust these nuts."

"You a damn fool, go check your mail cause the only way I'm going to go forward with this fraternity thing is if we go through it together."

"Yo, these envelopes look alike, let me see what they're talking about."

As soon as JayVon opened his envelope, his eyes widened with excitement.

"Yo, we're definitely doing this, this is on some exclusive, next level shit. Did you read all of the amenities we can get after we get accepted?"

"I did, which is why I want to cross the elite chapter, it could only boost our business even more, this may be the ticket we need to expand the store and maybe even open the adult theater we've been discussing."

"I think we should see if the other guys got the invitation as well, cause if they did, it's going to be like old times when we first crossed into BDM."

"They're actually on their way over to my crib now, so let's go."

"I'll meet you over there, I gotta shower and get this broad outta my house."

"Yo, when are you going to settle down? I thought you and Trice had something going on."

"We do but I think she's ready to settle down and I'm not sure I'm there yet, I think I love pussy too much to just be fuckin' one person for the rest of my life. Trice is cool though and our sexual chemistry is through the roof."

"If you say so, but hurry up, we don't have all day, we got real shit to do."

"Yea, yea, I'll be there in about twenty minutes, don't start the meeting without me."

***

Initiation

"OK gentlemen, I don't want to hold you too long, my brother and I received an invitation of sort from the fraternity to cross into elite, which would afford us funding for current as well as future businesses, even more connections in the fraternity and a laundry list of other perks, has anyone else received the invitation?"

"Yea, mine came in the mail yesterday, I was hoping I wasn't the only one that got it," Levi stated.

"Yeah, I got mine too," André, Julius and Daron said at the same time.

"This makes me breathe easier, now the question is, do y'all plan on crossing this time? Can we get a repeat from when we first crossed into Beta Delta Mu?"

"Hell yea," the rest of the guys said simultaneously.

"Bet, I'm going to send my application in today so they should get it by Monday and hope for the best."

Levi asked, "have you talked to Akira about it? This time is a little different from the last, you're married now and have a child."

"I know, I'm going to talk to her tonight, but I'm sure she won't have a problem with it."

"Well, I just did my app online so mine is in," JayVon said.

"Damn, I didn't even know it could be done online, let me go ahead and do mine now," Daron said.

"We right with you," Levi said, referring to him, Julius, and André.

"Well, damn, I guess I'll do mine tonight after I speak with Akira about it."

"Hit us in the group chat after you handle, we can go celebrate or something."

"Bet."

We dapped one another up and everyone left except for JayVon.

"What y'all got to eat in here, a brova hungrier than a mothafucka."

"When are you not hungry?"

"There's food in the fridge from last night that Akira made, help yourself."

"Bro, why are you always in my refrigerator?"

"Sis, what's good? I had a pretty lengthy workout this morning and I didn't have time to eat afterward cause your husband came and kidnapped me."

"Fair enough, hey love, how's your day?"
"I'm good baby, where's my son?"

"He's upstairs taking a much-needed nap."
"How's my nephew doing? I'm about to wake him up so we can play."

"You wake him up and he's staying with you tonight."

"I wouldn't mind that, I haven't spent much time with my nephew lately so I would welcome the company."

"Well, let me go pack his overnight bag and you and your nephew can spend as much time together as you'd like," Akira stated before walking out of the kitchen.

"Good looks on that bro, that gives me a chance to talk to Akira about crossing again, without JJ being a distraction or a witness to us arguing."

"That's what brothers and uncles are for, and let me know what time tomorrow afternoon or evening you want me to bring little man back home."

Just as Akira was bringing Jay my son's overnight bag, our doorbell rang.

"Heyyy girl, what are you doing on this side of town?"

"I came to see you and my nephew, where is he?"

"He's upstairs sleeping but JayVon is about to take him for the night."

"Jay's here?"

"Yeah, he's in the kitchen with Justice."

"If these ain't the finest twins I've ever seen, how are y'all?"

"Trice, what's good sis?"

"Hey beautiful, how are you?" Jay asked.

"I'm good, how are y'all doing?"

"We're good, can't complain, what are you doing in this neck of the woods?"

"I came to see my sis and nephew."

"Well, I'm about to take JJ with me for the evening, you're more than welcome to come along," Jay told Trice and winked at her.

"I just might take you up on that offer, I don't have anything planned for the evening."

"Bet, well, we can go grocery shopping and make it a date for three tonight."

"Sounds like a plan, now let me not be rude to my sis and go see her for a little while."

An Hour Later…

"Babe, can you come in here please, I have something I need to talk to you about."

"What's up?" Akira asked while walking into our family room.

"I got an invitation in the mail today from the fraternity to cross into the elites, I wanted to discuss it with you before I sent my application over."

"So, what is it going to entail?"

"I don't know yet but according to the invitation, there will be major perks to crossing again, funding for current and future businesses, more connections than we have access to now, and a bunch of other things, I think it'll be good for us."

"It damn sure sounds like it, I'd say go for it, it's only up from here, and when you do cross maybe you and the guys can expand the toy store and open the adult theater y'all been talking about before graduation."

"See, that's why I married you, you get me and we're on the same page, I'm going to submit my application online."

Initiation

"Let's get it baby."

"So, Mrs. Duarte, what are we going to do this evening since we have this big house to ourselves?"

"I can think of a few things we can do," she told me while straddling me.

"Keep it up and JJ's going to be promoted to big brother soon."

"That wouldn't be a bad thing, would it?" she asked me while planting small kisses on my neck.

"Not at all," I responded while gripping her ass and kissing her deeply.

"Well, let's get to making JJ a big brother."

Akira disrobed and the mere sight of her standing in front of me naked made my dick stand at attention. Now, Akira and I have always had great chemistry in and out of the bedroom but the only complaint I have with our sex life is the lack of special attention my dick gets from Akira's mouth.

Salt

I have never had a problem with eating her pussy. It brings me great joy to please my wife with my mouth, but sadly, I've never had the pleasure of knowing what Akira's mouth feels like on my manhood.

Akira straddled me and inserted my dick into her throbbing and wet pussy, all I could do was exhale deeply because being inside of her felt heavenly. She started riding me slowly, her titties bouncing up and down, I couldn't help but to grasp each one of them and suck on them gently. As she was grinding on my dick, her pussy muscles kept gripping my dick, she was tryin' to make me nut quick, but it wasn't happening, I planned on enjoying all of her for as long as she could tolerate. I stood up while still being inside of Akira, and started fuckin her while standing, and her moans, and screams let me know she was enjoying it thoroughly.

"Baby, I'm about to squirt all over your dick if you keep fuckin' me like this!"

Initiation

"Let her squirt baby, don't hold back, wet this dick all up."

"FUCKKKK! Jay baby!!" she screamed as she began squirting and an orgasm ripped through her body.

I laid her on the couch, she was breathing heavily because of the powerful orgasm that she just had. I placed my head in between her legs and feasted on her pussy like it was the best meal I've ever had. From the first kiss on the inside of her thighs to the first lick of her clitoris, another orgasm rocked her body, and I wasn't letting up. I kept my mouth on her, as orgasm after orgasm made her body shake uncontrollably, my tongue stayed on her clit, my hands gripping each of her breasts, I wasn't satisfied until she was satisfied, my queen had to get hers before I was going to get mine. I needed her to have at least seven orgasms before I even thought about getting mine and she was well past her seven and seeing the look of satisfaction on her face was all that I needed.

After the last orgasm rocked her body, I entered her tight, wet pussy again and gave her this r & b dick, that nice and slow grind, she matched every thrust of mine with one of her own, we were in sync, on one accord, and it felt so damn good. Right before I nutted, Akira turned from the missionary position and got on all fours, she wanted me to fuck her from the back. Seeing her ass jiggle as I was fucking her from behind was incredible, the way my dick disappeared in her pussy and was swallowed up by her ass, I was getting harder by the second.

"I want you to nut all over my face baby, can you do that for me?"

"Hell yea I can," I told her as I was digging her pussy out.

"I want you to smear your cum all over my face with your dick too baby."

"Got damn Akira! Turnover and catch all this cum baby! Ahhhhh!"

Initiation

I came all over Akira's face and just as she wished, I took my dick and painted her face with my cum. Ideally, I would have loved for her to suck my dick right after, but I knew if I would have asked, it would have been a problem and an argument to follow, so because we just had an awesome time enjoying one another, I decided to just live in the moment and enjoy the rest of the evening with my wife.

I went to the bathroom to clean up and grab a warm cloth for Akira's face and I heard my phone digging with a new email.

"Cone shower with me baby," Akira said to me.

I had just picked my phone up and placed it right back down. "Don't have that water on full hot Akira, you know you love having the shower water on hell."

"Stop being a baby, my shower water don't be that hot, you're over exaggerating," she said laughing.

"Lies and you know it, that's why you're laughing."

We showered and made love again, we were like two college students, not being able to keep our hands off one another.

Two Weeks Later…

As I was leaving the BDM adult toy store, I got an alert on my phone and it was an email from Brotha DipStick and it read, "Greetings Bro, I would like to personally thank you for replying to the initial email about crossing into Beta Delta Mu Elite, your credentials have been reviewed and I would like to invite you to the Elite informational which will be held at the Big Dick Mansion on Friday evening at seven p.m. please be on time. Also, please remember to use discretion as this is just like regular initiation, the less people know, the better, and as always, Beta Delta Mu business is always Beta Delta Mu business, nothing that is discussed amongst the brothers should be discussed amongst those who are not in the fraternity. Please respond to this email to acknowledge you have read the email in its entirety and agree to abide by all rules."

"This shit is about to be on some next level shit," I said aloud to myself.

When I got home, I let Akira know that elite initiation would be starting in two days.

"Babe, how was your day?"

"It was peaceful, me and the girls went out to eat and caught up with one another, took JJ to the park after he got out of school, and been doing some remodeling in the house, how was yours?"

"It was cool, just left the store, got the email letting me know that elite initiation is beginning on Friday, so if you have something to do, we may need to ask your parents to watch JJ since they'll be in town this weekend."

"I have no plans, some of the girls are coming over for a small game night so I'll be home, JJ will be no bother, you know he loves all his aunties."

"Bet," just as I was leaning in to kiss Akira, I heard my son's feet running into the living room from his playroom.

"Daddyyy!!!"

"There's my superstar! Did you have fun with mommy at the park"

"Yes!"

"What did you learn in school today?"

"I learned how to add, how to count to one hundred and I learned how to tie my shoes!"

"Good job son, you know daddy loves you, right?"

"Yes! And I love you too daddy!"

"Can I go see Uncle Jay tomorrow?"

"Let's call him and see if he's available tomorrow."

"Can I FaceTime him? I know how to do it."

"You sure can," I unlocked my phone and gave it to my son. He went right to my contacts, found JayVon's picture and facetimed him.

Initiation

"My favorite nephew! What's going on buddy?!"

"Hi Uncle Jay! Can I come see you tomorrow?"

"How about I come get you tonight and you can spend the night with me? Would you like that?"

"Yes! I'm going to pack my bag."

"Alright nephew, let me talk to your father please."

JJ handed me the phone before running to his room to pack his bag, with Akira right on his heels to help him.

"What's good brotha?"

"Ain't shit, did you get that email from the big bro?"

"Yea, right as I was locking up and leaving the store, I saw it."

"Have you been paying attention to the group chap?"

"I have too many groupers going on, I'll take a look at it after I shower."

"Cool, well, I'll be over in like ten minutes to get JJ."

"He'll be ready, as a matter of fact, I hear him running in here right now."

JJ ran and grabbed the phone from my hand, "I'm ready uncle Jay!"

"I'm on my way nephew, I'll see you in a little while, ok?"

"OK!"

"J, we need to link, just you and I before Friday so let me know when you're available."

"I'll come through tomorrow, I'll have Akira pick JJ up from school so I can shoot over to your place, and we can talk. Is everything alright?"

"Yea, everything is cool, just need to talk to you about the elite initiation, I just got some news about it and need to tell you about it."

"Aight, well, I'll come through tomorrow."

"Aight, well I'll see you in like two minutes, I'm around the corner."

After JayVon picked my son up I was hoping to have some alone time with Akira but to my surprise, she had plans tonight.

"Babe, I think I forgot to tell you that my girls and I are going out tonight."

"Yea you did, but you deserve a night out, so enjoy."

"What are you going tonight since you'll have the house to yourself?

"I need to get some work done, and I'll probably see what the rest of the guys are up to."

"Well, y'all behave yourselves tonight and I'll be back before midnight."

"Alright, love, stay safe and you behave yourself as well."

"I always do," she told me before kissing me.

"Now see, you know you about to start something that you're going to say you don't have time to finish."

"I don't know what you're talking about."

"Bullshit, but you know it's easy access cause you have that short dress on, we can get a quickie in before you have to leave."

"Baby, no, I'm not about to leave the house smelling like sex, no!"

"Akira, you got my dick hard now, don't leave me like this!"

She started planting kisses on my neck while massaging my dick through my basketball shorts. She pushed her hair to one side, lifted her dress, pulled her G-string to the side, and looked back at me and asked, "what are you waiting for?"

I took my already rock-hard dick out of my boxers, and slowly entered my wife. Tonight, she seemed like she was extra wet, and believe me, I was here for it all.

Initiation

"Now don't go making me make a mess like a few weeks ago, I have to go out," she told me.

"Nah baby, that mess you made was all your fault, but trust, I didn't mind it at all," I said to her while pulling her dress up more, so her beautiful breasts were exposed.

"Jay, I'm about to cum baby," she said to me, stuttering.

"Cum all over daddy's dick baby, wet him all up."

Three minutes later, we climaxed together, and it was perfect timing because just as we were cleaning ourselves up, the doorbell rang, it was Kiera, one of her friends from college coming to pick her up. I opened the door to let Kiera in, we hugged, and I told her Akira would be down in a minute.

"Y'all ain't slick, she told me she was ready when I spoke to her fifteen minutes ago," Kiera said laughing.

"Listen, I don't know what you're talking about, I think she had a stain or something on her dress that she was trying to get out."

"Yea, she had a stain alright, a stain of your man potion."

"I plead the fifth; get my wife back home safe and sound please and thank you."

"I got you bro, have you spoken to Levi today?"

"Nah, why what's up? Is everything alright with him?"

"Yea, he said something about having to fly back to Connecticut soon, something about the family, I thought he might've mentioned it to you or JayVon."

"Nah he didn't. I saw my brother earlier and he didn't mention anything to me either, I'll give L a call tonight to see what's up."

"Cool."

As I was sending Levi a text message, Akira was walking down the stairs.

Initiation

"Have a good night baby, I'll see you when I get home."

"Be safe and I'll be up waiting."

I kissed Akira before they left and went to boot up my computer. Just as I was getting some work done, my phone rings.

"Hey little man, what are you still doing up?"

"I miss you and mommy," my son said on the verge of tears.

"You're not having fun with your uncle J?"

"I am, can I stay with him tomorrow and not go to school?"

"Did uncle J say that would be alright with him?"

"Yes, he told me to ask you and mommy."

"Well mommy went out with your auntie Kiera, so I'm going to say it's alright, ok?"

"Thank you, daddy!"

"Oh, so I guess you're feeling better now?"

"Yup!"

I shook my head and started laughing, at such a young age my son knew how to get his way.

"Put your uncle on the phone."

"What up big bro?"

"How's your nephew treating you?"

"You know he loves me just as much as he loves you, we good over here."

"It's not a bother with him not going to school tomorrow, is it? I don't want to jam you up."

"Nah, nephew is always good over here, you home alone?"

"Yeah, what's up?"

"I wanted to tell you what I found out about the elite initiation, it's almost like when we were first pledging, but turned up to a whole different level."

"So basically, it's more fucking?"

"That, with some other freaky shit, and I heard that some of the women from Delta Pi Psi will be in attendance, kind of like as a replacement for the random broads we had to fuck and be around during our initial initiation."

"Why does Delta Pi Psi sound so familiar to me?"

"Think back, four years ago when we went to Connecticut for the weekend, the same weekend we found out we had more family up there, when we went to the party at ECU."

"Oh yea, now I remember, it's the sorority Akira was trying to pledge but never went through with it. So wait, we're going to be fuckin' chicks from Delta Pi Psi?"

"You got it, I heard they're like the female version of us, so you already know it's going to be crazy."

"Hell yea."

"Bro, you good? You look a little worried."

"Yea, you know after one or two of the initiation events I dipped 'cause it didn't feel right stepping out on Akira, but I'm married now, and I haven't slept with anyone else so I'm a little apprehensive now about going through with this."

"Bro, you'll be alright, just wrap it up, take on for the team, I heard it's really only one night, so after Friday or Saturday, you'll be good and so will we when we find out we've crossed into Elite Beta Delta Mu, get that gold added to our black and red para."

"I feel you; I'm still going to go through with it, just my nerves getting the best of me, that's all, we still in it to win it."

"That's the shit I like to hear! Well, I'm about to put neph in the shower, then we got mad stuff to do tonight, so we'll see you tomorrow."

"Aight bro, talk to you tomorrow."

"What the fuck have I gotten myself into? Akira is going to kill me if she ever finds out what is going down come Friday," I said to myself.

Two Days Later

"Baby girl, I'm on my way out, I probably won't be able to have my phone on me so prayerfully, nothing bad will happen."

"I forgot to tell you, I'm going out with the girls, so my parents are coming over to watch JJ for us, I meant to tell you the other night when I came in, but you distracted me."

"The lies you tell, you came home rather saucy and started fondling me, and that led me to rocking your pretty ass to sleep."

"I see you weren't complaining though, but back to the subject on hand, I told my parents they could stay in the guest room so JJ could sleep in his bed tonight, I didn't want them to have to make room in their hotel bed to accommodate him."

"That's cool with me, I'm going to hop in the shower and get ready so I can leave before they get here, you know your pops still doesn't care for me."

"I know, hopefully one day he'll get over his issues with you, it's not like I wasn't a willing participant in our sexcapades that resulted in me getting pregnant, but you know how he is, his image with his church members is everything and me getting pregnant out of wedlock somehow or another tainted his image; I'm shocked he still deals with me to be honest."

"You know he comes to visit and still talks to you because of your mother."

"You might be right about that, but go ahead and get ready, I'm going to shower after they get here so they can keep an eye on JJ."

"Alright love, listen, please be safe tonight and if you happen to get home before I do, text my phone to let me know you've made it home safely," I told her.

"I will my love."

I hopped in the shower really quickly, got dressed and made it out the door right before Akira's parents were able to park their car and get out. It amazes how this man will stand in his pulpit every Sunday and two other days during the week and teach love and forgiveness and can't or won't walk in love and forgiveness towards his only son-in-law. Either way, I'm not even keeping my mind on them, my focus is this elite initiation informational tonight and getting through the elite initiation.

When I got to the Big Dick Mansion, also known as the house Jay and I bought our first year at Atlanta University, all of my line brothers were outside, even our big brothers.

"What's good y'all, I know we're early, but are we that early?"

"Nah, we were waiting on you to get here so we could all go in together," André responded.

"Got it; so, am I the only one who is a little nervous about how all of this is going to play out?"

"Hell no," they guys responded collectively.

"Honestly though bro, you, Pussy Monster and Demon Dick will probably get a pass cause you're legacy, so I wouldn't even worry if I were you."

Salt

"Oh nah, I'm going to see this out till the end, I'm not going to bail on elite initiation like I did with the regular initiation, I'm in it with all my bros from start to finish this go round," I let him know.

"I respect it bro, on God I do; looks like they're ready for us," Brotha LDLT said.

We all walked into the Big Dick Mansion and to our surprise, it was transformed to look like a sex dungeon. It was getting hard just thinking about the memories I had in the house back in the day and the amount of sex that we were going to be doing with this elite initiation.

One of the OG brothers from BDM greeted us, "Welcome brothas to the elite initiation. We know we made you believe that tonight was going to be the informational for the Elite Beta Delta Mu chapter, but tonight is the night, one night of initiating and by tomorrow evening, you will receive an email letting you know whether or not you have been chosen. If by chance you happen to be one of the ones that didn't make the cut, just rest easy in knowing that you were able to fuck on a few different beautiful women tonight just for the hell of it, oh and my name is Brotha PYL, also known as Big Brotha Pipin' Your Lady."

Another OG stepped forward and introduced himself, "What's good fellas, my name is Big Brotha DHD, or Dickin' Her Down, we are going to get nastier than you called yourselves getting during your initial initiation process, tonight, we are fucking grown men style, each one of you will be paired up with two women from Delta Pi Psi sorority, I shouldn't have to tell y'all this but wrap your dicks up, I assume many of you are either married, in committed relationships or have a fuck buddies so we are not going to be raw doggin' anyone because that's nasty and disrespectful, and as Beta Delta Mu men, disrespect isn't something we do."

"Okay gentlemen, our ladies would like to remain anonymous so they have been disguised, their tattoos and other obvious marks that someone may recognize have been covered, if you receive oral, a condom must be on, no exceptions as just like yourselves, some of these women are married, in committed relationships or have steady partners. If at any time they say the code word fisting, that means you immediately stop whatever you're doing because they are uncomfortable, be respectful but in the same breath, show us what you got, tonight determines how much of a BDM man you really are and if you're cut out to be an Elite Beta Brotha, with that being said, find the door that has your names on it and let the fun begin," Brotha PYL stated.

"Oh, before you go, there are chains, handcuffs, whips, paddles, nipple clamps, vibes, dildos, leashes, and the list goes on. We won't be watching you, but we'll be listening out if anyone needs anything. Tonight is about endurance, and for us to see how far you're willing to go to become an Elite Beta Brotha, gentlemen, you are dismissed, let the fun begin."

Ironically enough, my room when I was living here was the room that had my name on it. I laughed to myself because I remember the first night of my initial initiation, those were some wild times. I entered the room and I saw two beautiful women on the bed, their bodies were making my favorite number, sixty-nine, as I watched them my dick grew harder and harder by the second. I undressed and watched them bring pleasure to each other for the betterment of fifteen minutes.

As they began squirting and climaxing simultaneously, I found myself nutting from their show. I went to the bathroom inside of the room and grabbed a warm wet cloth from each of them then cleaned myself up. When I got back to the room the ladies motioned for me to join them on the bed, and if you know me, you know I wasted no time in doing so.

Salt

One of the ladies, who looked as beautiful as midnight sky, took a condom, and put it on my dick with her mouth, the other began massaging my balls then started licking them while the other started giving me head. I've never been a quick nutter, but I'd be lying if I said I wasn't about to bust a nut, the mouth romance they were blessing me with had me going crazy, haven't had head like this since Akira and I briefly took a break some years ago and I kind of went on a fuckin' spree.

Anyhow, shorty who had my dick in her mouth motioned for the other chick to ride me, so she positioned herself on top of me, reverse cowgirl; she initially had to get used to my size, she kept easing herself onto me little by little, and with every inch of my dick that entered her, she would exhale slowly.

Once her pussy was full of my manhood, she began riding me slowly and the other shorty began licking her pussy and my balls all at the same time. Midnight took my dick out of her friend's pussy and started topping me off, whoever she was, she was talented as hell. Midnight was down for whatever, when her friend said the safe word, I took my hands off her waist and allowed her to catch her breath and regroup.

"Tie me up", Midnight told me.

I grabbed the cuffs from the side of the bed, and proceeded to cuff her hands together, then she told me, "Tie me all the way up." I then grabbed the bed restraints and tied her ankles to the bed; I also grabbed the ball gag and put it in her mouth, she shook her head 'no', so I took it out, then she said, "I want to be able to taste myself on you, so my mouth needs to be free."

I changed condoms and slowly entered Midnight, I was talking my time with her as I didn't know how her body would respond to me, but she was matching my every thrust, "fuck me harder," she said to me. I pulled her closer into me, but not so much as to hurt her, and I unleashed the true freak that was in me, her legs began shaking, and she began to scream because of the magnitude of the orgasm that ripped through her body.

"I want you in my ass," she told me.

"Say less." I untied her legs from the bed, she got on all fours, arched her back perfectly and inhaled deeply.

"You ready?"

She shook her head yes and I slowly inserted my dick into her tight ass. As I'm fuckin her I hear some of the other women in the other rooms and I kept hearing a voice that sounded exactly like Akira, and I know my wife's voice.

The lady's voice kept getting louder and louder and the louder she got, the more convinced I was that my wife was in another room fuckin and getting fucked by one of my frat brothers, I was beginning to get sick to my stomach. I quickly busted my nut inside of midnight's ass, cleaned myself off, gave her and her friend warm cloths so they could clean themselves up, quickly got dressed and got up out of there. I made it my business to quickly find one of the OG brothas to talk to them.

"Brotha Waterboi, is everything alright? You look like something is bothering you," DHD asked me.

"Nah, I swear I feel like my wife is here, are you sure there are only women from Delta Pi Psi here and no one else?"

"Positive, only ladies from Delta Pi Psi are here, is your wife a member of the sorority?"

"Nah, she tried to cross our freshman year in college, but she quit the line because she got pregnant, and to my knowledge, she never tried again or crossed."

"So technically there is a chance that she might've crossed, and you aren't knowledgeable of it?"

"Shit, I guess there could be a chance but I'm pretty sure I would've noticed her para after three years of being married."

"Bro, you know women hide shit a lot better than us men, so there could be a chance she crossed and never told you about it. We are not at liberty to divulge the identities of the ladies, but it's definitely a conversation you may need to have with your wife in the morning."

"Yeah, you're right big bro, thanks," I told him as I was making my way back to the room I was in."

"Brotha Waterboi, you can be excused for the evening, we know you're not in the right headspace to continue tonight, so we are excusing you for the evening, make sure you check your email over the weekend to see our decision."

"Thank you Brotha PYL, it was a pleasure meeting you both."

"The pleasure was all ours, you'll be seeing and hearing from us soon, get home safe."

On my way home I couldn't get Akira's voice out of my head, her moans, her screams, it was all too much for me. When I pulled into my driveway, I noticed she still wasn't home, which didn't ease my suspicions at all. I walked into the house and my mother-in-law was in the kitchen fixing herself a cup of tea.

"There's my favorite son-in-law, how are you doing?"

"Hey ma, I'm ok, how are you? How was your flight down here?"

"I'm doing well for an old woman; the flight wasn't too bad."

"Old woman where? How was JJ tonight? Hopefully he wasn't too much for you to deal with."

"You know it's been quite some time since I've had to deal with a toddler, he's got a hell of a lot of energy, but he wasn't a bother. We played with his race cars, went outside, and played tag and hide and seek, then I made dinner, he took his shower and went right to bed with no fuss. Speaking of dinner, your plate should still be warm, I wrapped it and put it in the oven for you, I didn't know what time you'd be back."

"Thanks ma, I appreciate it. Has Akira called or sent a text to say where she was or when she'd be back?"

"No, I haven't heard from her since she left, and she left maybe half an hour after you left."

"OK, thanks, I'm about to go hop in the shower, I'll be right back, that food smells amazing."

My mother-in-law and I sat up and talked until about two in the morning, and around two-thirty Akira came in.

"Hey baby, I'm shocked you beat me home, how was the informational tonight? Is the elite initiation something you're still thinking about going through with?"

"We actually didn't have the informational tonight, we had the actual initiation, I'm not sure I'm going to get in because I bailed earlier, wasn't feeling too well so a couple of the OG brothas told me to leave early and get my head straight."

"What happened? Is everything alright? I know this was something you were looking forward to."

"I'm good love, how was your evening? What did you and your girls end up getting into?"

I saw the look on her face, she was trying to come up with a lie on the spot, then she said, "My evening was pretty chill, we went bar hopping, sang karaoke, that's about it."

"You must've gone to a lot of bars, ya moms said you left not too long after I did."

"Nah, not really, when we got to the last bar, the one we were doing karaoke at, we got into a battle with some of the other people there, we were going song for song, we had fun. I'm about to hop in the shower, we can finish this conversation when I get out."

"I'm actually about to go to bed, I'm tired and not feeling too well."

"Do you need me to get you anything?"

"Nah, I'm good."

The fact that she was lying to me with a straight face was unbelievable; I didn't call her out on her bullshit because it was late, I was tired with a headache, and I didn't want us to start arguing and wake her parents or our son up, so I left it alone for the night. The next morning when I got up to shower, I noticed a Delta Pi Psi bracelet sitting on our bathroom sink, I shook my head and said aloud, "You've got to be fuckin' kidding me."

I showered and joined the rest of the family in the kitchen. "Good morning, Ma."

"Good morning, Justice, how'd you sleep last night?"

"Not great, still have that headache, but I'll be alright, I'm about to go to the gym."

"Hi daddy!!"

"There's my little man, how did you like spending the evening with your grandparents last night?"

Initiation

"It was fun! Grandpa said I can come to his house for a whole week, when can I go?"

"I don't have a problem with it son, but you can ask your mother."

"Are you eating breakfast this morning?" Akira asked me as she was making JJ's plate.

"Nah, I'm not hungry, I just need to go to the gym and workout."

"OK, what time do you think you'll be back?"

"I'm not sure, can you walk with me to the car?"

Akira and I walked to my car in silence, she folded her arms across her chest as if she had an attitude. "What's up?

I pulled her bracelet out of my pocket, "When did you pledge Delta Pi Psi?"

"Fuck," she said under her breath.
"The year after I had JJ, because I had started the process, I didn't have to go through the full process to complete my initiation."

"Akira, why the fuck would you hide this from me?"

"I don't know, maybe because of the hell I gave you when you crossed Beta Delta Mu, I felt like a hypocrite, and I didn't want you to throw it back in my face."

"Wow, is that what you think I would have done? I would have loved to be at your probate to support you, it's like I don't know who you are anymore; what other secrets are you hiding from me?"

"No more secrets, I promise you, I'm sorry Justice," she said crying.

"I need some time to digest this, I'll be at my brother's house for a while."

"Fair enough, I can't even be mad at you for it."

"Question, Trice, Kiera, Jade, Kyra, and Marie, are they all your line sisters?"

Initiation

"Yea, we all stayed in the same dorm and became friends before we decided to cross, but yes, they are my line sisters."

"Am I the only one that didn't know you are in Delta Pi Psi?"

"As far as I know, none of the ladies have told anyone, I made them promise they wouldn't because I wanted to be the one to tell you when the time was right, so none of your brothers know either."

"Ok, I'll be here in the morning to pick JJ up and bring him to school, I don't have the energy to deal with this information and your parents, more so your father, right now, so I'll be back when they leave."

"Justice, I never met to hurt you, lie to you or embarrass you, I promise that was never my intention."

"Were you a part of the women who were at the BDM elite initiation last night?"

She put her head down and began sobbing uncontrollably, no words needed to be said, I knew I wasn't bugging last night, I know my wife's voice.

"We were able to see the guys, but they couldn't see our faces and you know any identifying marks or tattoos we had were covered…"

I interrupted her and asked, "Akira, what are you trying to tell me?"

"You know I'm ovulating this week and somehow in the midst of everything last night, the condom came off and…"

"Who were you fuckin last night, Akira?"

"I don't want to tell you because I feel like if I do tell you, it's going to end our marriage."

"Was it one of my line brothers?"

"He's a little more than just your line brother."

"So it was either Levi or JayVon, so you were fucking my cousin or my brother? Like my blood brother? My twin? Which one was it?"

"It was Jay."

"Oh fuckkkk no!! You are not sitting here telling me that you were fucking my brother!"

"I had no control over it, we were all trying to get placed with our significant others, but they weren't having it, Justice, baby, you have to believe me, you know you're the only one who has had my heart since the day we met, you know I would never step out on you, but last night was out of my control."

"I'm out, I'll be back in the morning to get my son."

I couldn't believe this, my wife, and my brother. I know Jay would never look at my wife inappropriately let alone ever think about sleeping with her, and I know he didn't know it was her because he would have objected to it immediately. I have to tell him, as much as I don't want to, but I know shit like this can't stay a secret, especially since Akira is ovulating this week, and there could now be a question mark as to which one of us is the father, if she indeed get pregnant at all yesterday.

I got to my brother's house in five minutes flat, broke all the speeding limits and ran more than a few red lights. I had to talk to him, and this shit couldn't wait. When I got to his place, Trice was just leaving.

"Hey bro, you good?"

"What's good sis, I've been better. Have you talked to Akira today?"

"Nah, not yet is everything alright?"
"I'll let her talk to you about it if she chooses to."

"Sounds serious, she's at the house?"
"Yea, you know her parents are in town, right?"
"I didn't know that I haven't seen them in years, I'm going to swing by there now before I head to work."

"Aight, sis, I'll see you later."

Trice and I hugged before I went in to see my brother.

"What's good chief? Is everything alright?"
"Nah, far from alright. How was last night?"

"You asking me like you weren't there with me, it was crazy."

"I bailed early."
"Why? What happened? Is JJ alright?"

"Yes, he's good, my in-laws are in town, they watched him last night, what do you have to drink? I need something strong, and you will too when I tell you this crazy shit."

"Oh lord, what the fuck done happened now?"

"Your sister-in-law was there too."

"Wait, what the hell was Akira doing there? I thought I was Delta Pi Psi women only?"

"It was, apparently, Akira crossed the year after she had JJ, you know were on again and off again and weren't really communicating like that, she hid it from me and her parents; I wouldn't have known if I didn't see her DPP bracelet in the bathroom this morning, she never would have told me."

"Is that why her, Trice and the others are so close, are they all in the sorority together?"

"Yup."

"That's crazy bro, I'm sorry you have to deal with this and find out that way. Wait, who was she with last night and how did you find out?"

"So, she gets loud, and you know I know my wife's voice, so as I'm doing my thing in the room, I keep hearing Akira's voice, which started making me sick, to know someone else was in another room inside of my wife."

"I can't even imagine; did she tell you who it was?"

"Take a drink with me, it's about to get a lot heavier when you hear this."

We took four shots of whiskey to the face before I dropped the bomb on my brother.

"You."

"Me what?" Jay asked, confused.

"Akira was with you last night, I'm not sure who the other chick was, but Akira was one of your girls last night."

Jay became weak in the knees and looked like he was going to be sick.

"That's not funny Justice, seriously, who was she with last night?"

"You know I wouldn't bullshit you, Jay; it was you. She told me before I came over here. Apparently, the ladies could see us, but we couldn't see them. At first, I thought it was Levi cause she was like it was someone close to me, then she told me it was you," I told him, pouring myself another drink.

"Jus, you know I would never, and I do mean never disrespect you or your marriage like that bro, you know that's not even my style, and you know I would never think about ever stepping to Akira, on our parents grave."

Salt

"I know you wouldn't; I'm not even upset with you, I'm more upset with her for not telling me that she crossed Delta Pi Psi, had I known prior to this morning, last night would have never happened. I don't understand why she would hide something like that from me, it makes me wonder what else she may be hiding."

"You know my place is your place so if you need to stay here for a while to get your mind right, it's not a problem."

"You haven't heard the worst of it yet."

"I don't think I can take anything worse than what you just told me, but drop it on me," he said, taking the rest of the whiskey in the bottle to the face.

"Out of all the weeks for us to have the elite initiation, it had to be the week she's ovulating, and she said something about the condom coming off somehow when y'all were in the room."

Jay's knees buckled and he lost his balance and fell to the couch.

Initiation

"I think I'm going to be sick, this shit is too much, ain't no fuckin' way. How soon till she finds out if she's pregnant and who the father is?"

"Hopefully within the next two weeks; I'm going to stay here until Friday, her parents are still in town, and you know her father still can't stand me, and I really don't feel like dealing with that man on top of dealing with Akira and all of her secrets. This shit is too much."

"Say no more, you know I'm here for you. Do any of the other guys know?"

"Hell no, I just found out this morning; let's keep this between us, please."

"Say less, I got you."

Two months later

"So, I took a pregnancy test, and I am pregnant, I have my first doctor's appointment on Tuesday at two in the afternoon."

"Ok, I'll move some things around and make sure I'm there, did you ask them about doing a paternity test?"

"Yea, they said they'd do it, I guess they have to draw my blood and do a cheek swab for you to match it with the baby's DNA."

"Ok, good. We haven't discussed this but in the event the baby isn't mine, what do you want to do?"

"Honestly, I don't know, I've been going back and forth with that decision, I was hoping we could decide together, what are your thoughts?"

"Neither one of us believes in abortion, and if by chance Jay is the father, I know he would want to be in the baby's life, maybe this is something the three of us should discuss."

"I agree, why don't you call him."

I facetimed my brother, this was a conversation that I wasn't mentally ready for.

"Fam, what's good?"

"So, Akira and I were just talking, she took a pregnancy test, and she is pregnant. Her first appointment is Tuesday afternoon, they're going to do the DNA test while we're there and hopefully a week or two after we'll get those results."

"Ok," Jay breathed deeply, then said, "what are you going to do if by chance the baby is mine?"

"Well, that's why we called you," Akira said, "we want to know what your thoughts are on this situation."

"I've been trying to think about every outcome of this mess, I mean, if the baby is mine, I'd no doubt be there and be in his or her life, but I feel like the ultimate decision is yours Akira, I mean, you're the one carrying the baby, so it kinda boils down to what you want to do."

Akira sighed deeply and began crying then said, "How about we make a decision, if there's a decision to be made, after we get the test results back, once we have a definitive answer we can then move forward, but until then, I think we should just wait."

"Fair enough," Jay said, then added, "let me know how the appointment goes when y'all are done on Tuesday; oh and Justice, please check our group chat, we have some things to discuss."

"We got you bro, and I'll catch up when we end the call, I'm terrible at keeping up with the groupers."

"True indeed you are, but I'll holla at y'all later, Trice is on her way over."

"Aight bro, we'll talk to you later."
"Him and Trice getting pretty serious, aren't they?"

"I don't know about all of that, I do know Trice is ready to settle down and she has some real strong feelings for Jay, but I don't know if that's where his head is at, you know he's never been the type to be a one-woman man," Akira told me.

"I think there's some strong feelings on his part too, but you know Jay, it's going to take Trice to stop messing with him altogether for him to profess his feelings for her, remember that's what you had to do to me to get me to act right."

"I do remember," she said, laughing hard. It felt good to see and hear Akira laughing, these past couple of months have been nothing but arguments, the silent treatment and pure tension in the house, I just pray we can get through this and hope the baby she is carrying is mine and not my brothers, I'm not sure I'd be able to stay with her if the baby turned out to be my nephew instead of my child.

"How are you feeling?"
"Pretty damn good, surprisingly. This baby is treating me better than JJ did when I was pregnant with him."

"Do you remember when you used to text me at crazy times of the night because you wanted food or something and I had to find what you were craving and a delivery service to get it delivered to you?"

Salt

"Yea, I remember, I always felt like I was driving you crazy."

"You were but it was all worth it because we got a perfect little boy out of it."

"True indeed we did."

"Listen, I want to take you out tonight, just you and I, we haven't had a date night in what seems like forever, and I think we're long overdue for it, what do you say?"

"I'd love that very much, who's going to watch JJ?"

"I'm going to see if one of the guys can watch him, I'm sure it'll be no problem, go ahead and start getting ready, I'll take care of JJ," I told her then kissed her on her forehead.

I sent a text message to our group chat to see if any of the guys were available to kick it with their nephew for a few hours. Everyone responded except Jay, which I expected because I knew he was kicking it with Trice. I told them if they all wanted to come through and spend the evening with my son, they were more than welcomed to, they said they'd be at the house in about forty-five minutes, which was perfect because it gave me enough time to get JJ showered, fed, and get myself together.

When Akira finished getting ready, she was glowing, she was wearing her hair in its natural state, she had it half up and half down with two small pieces hanging on either side of her face, she was wearing a form fitting black dress that hugged every curve of her body and it accentuated her small protruding belly, she was just beginning to show a little bit and it was the sexiest sight to me, I missed seeing her glowing when she was pregnant with our son because I was living in Georgia and she was in Connecticut, so being able to witness this right now, it was one of the best feelings ever.

"Baby girl, you look absolutely stunning."

"I feel as fat as a cow but thank you baby."

"There isn't anything fat about you, other than your ass, but that's always been there," I told her playfully tapping her on her butt.

"So, Mr. Duarte, where are we off to tonight?"

"I figured we would take it old school, taking you to where we had our first date the first time you came to Georgia to visit me, do you remember where that was?"

"I sure do, the arcade, I think it was called something like Main Event or something like that?"

"Yea, then after that we're going to dinner, then dancing and I figured we could take a drive, to watch the sun set and just enjoy one another."

"What's gotten you in such a good mood lately?"

"Honestly? I'm tired of all of the arguing, fighting, and tension that's been between us lately, if I could redo the night of the elite initiation, I would in a heartbeat. Something in my gut was off that night and I couldn't place my finger on what it could have been, I also wish I could have been there for you during your probate, I missed a major event in your life, and it's been fuckin' with me since the day you told me you were in Delta Pi Psi. Going forward, I want to be a better husband to you, I don't know exactly where we fell off, but we need to get us back, that fun, loving couple who were so in love with one another it hurt when we were apart; I need that for us."

Tears began creeping down her face, and she said, "Justice, baby, I want to apologize for leaving you out of one of the most important days of my college career, I missed having you at my probate, if I could go back and do it all over, I would in a heartbeat. It was hard enough doing it under the radar so my parents wouldn't find out, I felt like if I would've told you, everything would've spiraled out of control for me. With us still taking a break from one another but expecting our first child together, that in itself was a lot for me to deal with, there was nothing more in this world I wanted than to be with you and JJ under one roof, it was tough going to doctor's appointments by myself and not knowing if you were going to make it back in time to watch me give birth. I went through a lot of depression while I was pregnant with JJ and I always promised myself that when I got pregnant again, I wouldn't allow anything or anyone to stress me out and I would focus on being happy for the duration of the pregnancy, so no matter what the results read come Tuesday, you have to do what you feel is best for you because I'm keeping my baby. I don't know if he or she will be yours or JayVon's, but one thing I do know is that they will be my baby, one that I'm falling in love with every day that passes. We can get back to that love we once had for one another, I just think it's going to take some time, but we can and will come back to that."

I stepped in front of my wife, put my hand on her growing belly, then bent over to kiss it, then

Initiation

I embraced my wife for what seemed like an eternity, she knew she had me for life, and I knew the same about her. We've weathered many storms together and this was just another test we had to pass to prove our love for one another.

"I don't want you to think for one second that I don't love you Akira, because I do, and no matter what the results read on Tuesday or whenever we get the results back, we have a baby on the way and the only concern of mine is that the baby is born healthy, nothing else matters and that's my word."

"Justice, there's something else I need to tell you, it's not bad but since we're in a pretty good space right now, I feel like now is the appropriate time to tell you this."

"Do I need to sit for this? Is it bad news?"

"It's not bad news, but it's something I should've told you when I told you that I pledged Delta Pi Psi."

Aww fuck, here we go, I can only imagine what's about to come out of her mouth, I almost don't even want to know.

"So, you know how when we got back together after I had JJ and after graduation, I didn't have to look for a job and I haven't had a job since I've graduated college?"

"Yea, what about it? You said your parents left you some time of trust fund that you couldn't access until you graduated college and that's how you've been getting by, was that another lie?"

"Kinda, so, Trice, Kiera, Marie, Jade, Kyra and I own a swinger's club, The DyNasty Pleasure Palace."

I began laughing, I swear she was about to tell me something bad. I was upset that she's been hiding shit from me for all these years, but I'm actually proud of her.

"What the fuck is so funny Justice?"
"I'm laughing because I honestly thought you were going to tell me something terrible like you slept

with another one of my frat brothers or something, you were about to give me a heart attack. Akira, how did we get to a place where you feel or felt as if you had to hide stuff from me?"

"I don't know, but I promise, you know everything now, no more secrets, that's the last thing I was hiding from you, you have my word on that."

"Baby, I'm proud of you, but a swingers club though? I'm not even mad at it, I'm proud of you my love, now when are we going to The DyNasty Pleasure Palace so I can experience it?"

"Half past never, I will not be sharing you with anyone else."

"Let's go baby girl, the guys are here and we're going out to have fun, then come home and have some more fun, if you know what I mean," I said and winked at her.

We kissed JJ and told him that we'd see him in the morning because we were going to be getting home late, we also told him to behave for his uncles.

"Justice, let me holla at you before you leave," Levi said.

"What's up bro?"
"Has Akira spoken to Kiera lately or mentioned anything to you about Kiera?"

"Nah, she hasn't said anything, and she hasn't mentioned speaking to Kiera lately, why, is she alright?"

"Yea, she's good, just found out some shit about her though, and I'm not sure if I can stomach it or continue to be with her after this shit I just found out."

"What the hell happened?"
Levi inhaled deeply and exhaled slowly then said, "You remember Big Brothas PYL and DHD?"

"Yea, from the elite initiation, what about them?"

"Evidently, Kiera has been with both of them. When she crossed Delta Pi Psi at ECU, during her initiation process, she had to fuck some of the guys from Beta Delta Mu, and coincidently, those two brothers were PYL and DHD, she told me a few weeks ago and I haven't been right since. I know it was before we made it official, but the fact that two of my frat brothers were with my girl, it's just not sitting right with me."

"Damn cuz, I'm sorry to hear that, what are you going to do?" I know I could've told him about the whole situation with Akira and JayVon, but I wasn't trying to relive that tonight and I don't know how he would've reacted to it, we haven't told anyone and I'm not sure we ever should.

"I'm not sure what I'm going to do yet, but I don't want to hold you up, I know Akira is waiting on you."

"Yo, I'm going to hit you up tomorrow and we can really talk about this, I kinda know what you're going through, but we're going to like tomorrow and talk this out."

"I appreciate it fam, I really do, and I want to marry her crazy ass, but we'll talk about that tomorrow."

We dapped it up, Levi went back in the house to join the other guys and my wife, and I went on our way. I was conflicted on whether or not I should say something to Akira or not about her line sister, Kiera, but it wasn't my place and it got me to thinking that if Kiera was fucking Beta men during her initiation, I'm wondering if Akira was doing the same back then as well.

"Baby, you alright? Looks like something is bothering you."

"I'm good love, just replaying the conversation I just had with Levi; have you spoken to Kiera lately?"

"Yea, we talk every day in our group chat, is everything alright with her?"

"Yea, she's good."
"Is Levi alright?"

"He will be fine, I'm going to go see him tomorrow and talk to him; but enough about them, tonight is our night to reconnect and have fun."

A Week Later

"Justice, the doctor just emailed me the results of the paternity test, I haven't opened it yet."

"Whatever the results read, you know I'm not going anywhere, whether that little one is mine or my niece or nephew, I'm going to be right by your side no matter what."

Akira clicked the link in the email and read the results out loud.

"Baby Duarte has matched ninety-nine-point nine nine percent to Justice Duarte."

"Thank you, God," I said aloud.

Akira cried and so did I. Once we got ourselves together, I sent a text message to my brother letting him know the results, and to say he was elated would be an understatement.

"Cigars and two shots to celebrate," he replied via text.

I picked Akira up and carried her up the stairs to our bed, gently laid her on the bed and began undressing her.

"Babe, I'm going to be late picking JJ up."
"Shhh, let me do what I do, we'll pay the extra for being a little late."

I planted small kisses from her feet up to her inner thighs, then I let my tongue do what it wanted to do and go where it wanted to go, and it went straight for her pussy. I gently licked the inside of her pussy then put my whole mouth on her, I wanted to taste all of her and make her scream my name.

The longer I kept my mouth on her, the more tense her orgasms got, and the more her body shook with orgasms, the harder my dick got.

"Justice, you gotta let me up, my body can't take it anymore; you're not playing fair," she moaned.

"Oh, so you don't want this dick that's waiting for you?"

"I do baby, but the things you were doing to me with your mouth was almost too much, but I'm ready for that dick daddy."

I went into her extremely wet pussy slowly, being inside of her felt like what I imagine heaven to be like.

"Justice, please go slow baby, I don't want to hurt the baby."

"I got you ma."
I gave her slow but deep strokes, and I could already tell I wasn't going to last long, her pussy was so wet, I was going to bust quick.

"J, cum with me baby, I'm about to cum all over your dick," she said as her legs began to shake.

"I'm cumming with you baby, Ahhhhh!!"
"Damn baby, that was great."

Just as we were cleaning ourselves up, JJ's school called to let us know we were five minutes late in picking him up and to make sure someone was on their way. I assured them that I was on the way and that I had no problems paying the late fee, it was well worth it, cause Akira and I needed the release I just provided for the both of us.

As I was putting JJ in his car seat I got an email from Big Brotha DHD, it read, "Hello good brothers, I hope this email finds you well. I first want to apologize for the delay in getting back to you all about the elite initiation, there were some things that happened that we could not have foreseen, and for that, we apologize. I want to extend my personal congratulations to you for being chosen as a brother of Beta Delta Mu Elite, you can now proudly rock the Black, Red & Gold. Please reply to this email whether or not you accept the invitation, we look forward to hearing from you."

I sent my reply right back, then sent a message to our group chat to see who else got the same message. All of the guys replied that they got the message, and they had all sent their replies in as well, it was official, we were all members of Beta Delta Mu Elite.

As I was pulling up to the house, I got a message from an unknown sender.

"Kira! We're home, JJ is in his room, I have to run back out," I yelled to her before going back to my car to open the message. I sat in my car and opened the message, it was a video of Akira suckin' some guys dick and looking like she was really into it.

"What the fuck is this? This chick won't suck my dick, has never sucked my dick and she's out here suckin' some random dude? If this ain't the bullshit!"

I was blindsided by her pledging Delta Pi Psi and found out on some bullshit, but this right here, I'm not sure if we can bounce back from this.

I started my car, backed out of the driveway, and sent the video to Akira, along with a message that read, "What's done in the dark always comes to light. To say I'm disappointed would be an understatement, I don't even know who you are anymore, you are not the same woman I married. I'll be gone for a while, not sure how long but I need to get my mind right before coming back home."

After five minutes, she replied, "OMG baby, it's not what you think, I can explain, just please let me explain…"

COMING SOON…

Rebel: Akira's Story

www.ingramcontent.com/pod-product-compliance
Lightning Source LLC
Chambersburg PA
CBHW030333020726
47493CB00004B/1263